MURDER
in the
Choir

Pippa Parker Mysteries: 2

Liz Hedgecock

WHITE
RHINO
BOOKS

Copyright © Liz Hedgecock 2017

All rights reserved. Apart from any use permitted under UK copyright law, no part of this publication may be reproduced, stored in a retrieval system, or transmitted, in any form or by any means, electronic, mechanical, photocopying, recording or otherwise, without the prior written permission of the copyright owner.

This is a work of fiction. Names, characters, businesses, places, events and incidents are either the products of the author's imagination or used in a fictitious manner. Any resemblance to actual persons, living or dead, or actual events is purely coincidental.

ISBN-13: 978-1976752155

For Stephen,
who cooks a mean schnitzel

Gadding Messenger
November 18, 2016

MUM HELPS POLICE SOLVE LOCAL MURDER

Most mothers-to-be start taking it easy when they approach their due date. One local mum, however, opted for a different strategy, assisting police in solving the murder of well-known Much Gadding resident Barbara Hamilton, who was found dead at Gadding Goslings playgroup earlier this month.

Pippa Parker, who recently moved to Much Gadding with her family, volunteered to wear a listening device and recorded the confession of the accused while at a playgroup meeting. A close friend revealed to this newspaper that Mrs Parker went into labour at the same time and was subsequently rushed to hospital. We understand that mother and baby have returned home and are doing well. Mrs Parker also has a two-year-old son.

Inspector Fanshawe of Gadcestershire Police states: 'We are grateful to Mrs Parker for her assistance with this case. While we would not advise expectant mothers to become involved in active police operations, all help from the public is appreciated. Mrs Parker was very brave and she did a fantastic job. We hope she enjoys some time off with her new arrival.'

Mrs Parker was unavailable for comment.

Gadcester Chronicle
November 20, 2016

Opinion

MULTITASKING MUM FIGHTS CRIME

by Janey Dixon

I don't know about you, but I find it tough just getting through the things I need to do in a day.

Some people, however, are different.

Take Much Gadding resident Pippa Parker, 39, who recently helped police to catch the killer of Barbara Hamilton. She took multi-tasking to a new level by running the local playgroup at the same time as wearing a wire and luring the murderer into providing a full confession. Oh, and if that wasn't enough she also went into labour, hitching a ride in a cop car to the hospital just in time to deliver her baby.

We take our hats off to Mrs Parker, who is no doubt whipping up a cake and reading *War and Peace* to the baby whilst knitting socks with her feet and recording a single for charity. That is possibly why she was unavailable for comment.

CHAPTER 1

Pippa Parker gazed at her sleeping baby. It had taken half an hour of feeding, burping, rocking, and singing that stupid song from kids' TV, but at last Ruby was in her cot, tiny fists balled, her dark eyelashes fluttering with each breath.

Freddie was in the sitting room, watching a *SuperMouse* DVD. Again. Pippa suspected she ought to feel guilty, but it was Freddie's first screen time that day, and it was mid-afternoon. So no, she didn't. Not with the prospect of twenty minutes of peace and quiet.

She could make a meal plan for next week. Or find that working-from-home website she'd heard about. She could definitely have a hot cup of tea.

Pippa crept downstairs, thanking her lucky stars that they weren't at Rosebud Cottage any more. You could have cast those stairs in a horror movie, they creaked so ominously. Laurel Villa, their still-new home, had a broad, shallow staircase carpeted in beige, which hid the noise but not the stains. *Perhaps when both the kids were at school*, she mused, eyeing the already-speckled pile. *Good God, Pippa, stop wishing your life away!*

Pippa entered the kitchen and flicked on the kettle, and her eye snagged on her library book, waiting on the worktop. *The Mysterious Affair At Styles*. Yes, it was the umpteenth time she'd read it, but that didn't matter. The bookmark poked its tongue out at her, a direct challenge which she couldn't resist. Pippa stretched her hand towards it and —

Ding-dong!

Oh no. Not again.

Pippa peered into the hall. The winter sun threw a shadow onto the wall. A shadow whose arm was reaching for the doorbell.

A Sheila-shaped shadow.

'Noooo!' Pippa ran across the hall and flung the door open.

'Oh, hello Pippa,' Sheila beamed. 'I was just passing.' It was the third time she had been just passing that week, which was remarkable since Sheila lived on the opposite side of the village, and it was only Thursday. 'Where's Ruby?' A line appeared between her eyebrows.

'Sleeping in her cot.' Pippa put a hand on the doorframe. 'I put her down two minutes ago. It took ages to get her off.'

The kettle pinged. 'Just in time for tea, then!' Sheila put a foot over the threshold and Pippa had no choice but to draw back.

A crackle, and a magnified robot 'Waaaaaaaa' erupted from the baby alarm.

'There she goes,' sighed Pippa. 'You know where the cups are, Sheila.' She closed the door and ran upstairs. Ruby was turning from side to side and waving her fists in the air, her eyes screwed up tight. 'Shhhh, Ruby, shhhh.'

She stroked the baby's head. 'Shhhh...' Ruby's movements slowed. She opened her eyes, looked at Pippa very solemnly, and her eyelids began to close.

Could it be...?

'Here she is!' called Sheila, from the doorway. Ruby's eyes popped open. Sheila walked past Pippa and tickled Ruby under the chin. Ruby opened her mouth and a strange yelp came out. 'Ruby-poos has woken up specially for Granny, hasn't she?'

Ruby was smiling, and her little hands were stretching for a pick-up. 'Come on then,' sighed Pippa, leaning into the cot. 'No rest for the wicked.'

'She's not wicked, are you Ruby?' cooed Sheila. 'No she isn't!' She held out a finger and Ruby closed her hand around it, waving it like a prize. 'No she isn't!'

'Let's go and say hello to Freddie.' Pippa scooped Ruby up and bore her downstairs into the sitting room. 'Sheila, could you make the tea?'

Sheila held her hands out, much as Ruby had done. 'Here, I'll hold her. I never remember where you keep everything.' She bounced Ruby on her knee. 'Hello, Freddie,' she said.

'Hello Granma,' Freddie replied, his eyes not leaving the screen.

Pippa topped up the kettle, switched it on again, and fetched Sheila's china cup and saucer.

'Can I have a snack, Mummy?' yelled Freddie.

'Not if you shout like that,' Pippa replied, peering into the biscuit tin. Someone had eaten all the bourbons and left the custard creams. *Oh well.* She took it through and put it on the coffee table. 'No more than two, Freddie. You'll spoil your dinner.'

'And what is Ruby eating now?' Sheila asked.

'Er, milk?'

'Is that all?' Sheila lifted Ruby into the air and made a shocked face at her. 'She'll float away!'

'She's three months old, Sheila. That's what the books say. And the health visitor.'

'Oh, books.' Sheila blew a raspberry at Ruby. 'Who cares about silly old books?'

The kettle pinged and Pippa escaped to the kitchen. 'I care about you,' she told the book on the worktop, as she poured water into the cups. 'I just don't get time to read you.' Perhaps when Simon came home she could run a bath and take the book with her. Oh, a bath… She imagined sinking into the bubbles, adding hot water every so often, turning a page, then another…

'And what have we been doing today?' called Sheila.

Pippa added milk and took the cups through. As soon as she had put them on the coffee table, Sheila passed Ruby back to her. 'Well, we went to playgroup this morning, and then we came home for lunch, and, um, I did some washing…' Was that really all she'd done? She felt as if she had run a marathon while juggling. Sheila's eyes were roving round the room, lingering on the pile of magazines by the armchair, the toys on the floor, the mug on the bookshelf which she must have missed earlier. 'Of course, we've been busy sorting out preschool. Freddie starts next week.'

'Preschool?' Sheila looked horrified. 'Already?'

'He's three. Lots of his friends go —'

'It seems so *early* to be packing him off.' Sheila put her cup down and opened the biscuit tin.

'It's two mornings a week, Sheila. We were lucky to get

a place. It just happened that a vacancy came up, and we were next on the list. If we'd turned it down, who knows when another place would have become free.'

'Mmph.' Sheila selected a custard cream and took a precise bite. 'It sounds like a child factory.'

'Sheila!' Pippa jerked her head towards Freddie.

'We didn't have this in my day.' Sheila pecked at her biscuit. 'I had the boys with me until they started school. Once you get them into a routine, it's easy.'

I'm sure it would be, thought Pippa, *if certain people didn't keep turning up at nap time.* 'As I said, Sheila, it's two mornings a week. Freddie's friends are there, it will get him ready for school, and Ruby and I can have time together too.'

'Well, they're your kids.' Sheila sighed. She picked up her cup and sipped her tea. 'And of course with only one at home it's much easier for you. You can start getting the house straight. Maybe buy yourself a slow cooker. I used to swear by mine…' Her eyes glazed over.

'Indeed.' Pippa balanced Ruby carefully and leaned to get her tea. It was warm. Ish. 'And now Ruby's sleeping longer, you'll be able to babysit.'

'Oh, of course. When the time comes. I wouldn't want you to disrupt her feeding. And I do have a lot of commitments, you know. I couldn't drop them on a whim.' Sheila drained her cup. 'Good heavens, look at the time. It's my turn to host bridge club and I have nothing in the house.'

'Oh dear,' said Pippa.

'Bye-bye, Ruby-poos!' Sheila stroked Ruby's cheek with her forefinger. 'Granny has lots and lots to do, but she'll be back soon, just see if she isn't!' She got up. 'I'll take this cup to the kitchen for you. To save time.'

'Thank you so much,' Pippa said to her back. She pushed herself up from the sofa with her free hand, and Ruby crowed as she rose into the air. 'Freddie, say goodbye to Grandma.'

'Bye Granma!' shouted Freddie, engrossed in the closing credits of *SuperMouse*.

'And what are we doing for the rest of the day?' Sheila picked up the library book and wrinkled her nose. 'Agatha Christie?'

'We'll probably go for a walk. I need a couple of things from the shop, and Freddie will enjoy a run out.'

'Good.' Sheila replaced the book on the worktop, exactly square. 'Much healthier than this detective nonsense. Didn't Agatha Christie go out with the ark?'

'They're classics, Sheila.' Pippa felt herself heating up.

Sheila laughed dismissively. 'If you like that sort of thing, who am I to judge? I suppose it keeps your mind active. At least it isn't real-life murders.' She shuddered. 'We've had quite enough of that in Much Gadding. Anyway.' Pippa stood back to let her pass. 'Bye-bye, Ruby.' Sheila leaned down to plant a kiss on the baby's forehead. Ruby looked confused. 'See you soon!'

'Bye, Sheila.'

'Oh yes, goodbye Pippa. Don't forget to wrap Ruby up, it's very chilly out there.'

Pippa stood in the doorway and watched Sheila's car inch down the drive. While the walk had been a spur-of-the-moment invention, it was probably a good idea. Ruby might fall asleep. Freddie would enjoy a play on the village green. He could feed the ducks. She could sit on a bench. Perhaps, if the planets aligned, read a chapter or two of her book. Her eyes prickled, and she blinked, once, twice.

Ruby had slept badly the previous night, and Pippa had spent most of playgroup feeding, rocking, feeding, settling... She had exchanged perhaps ten words with Lila, who was texting on her phone, a secret little smile on her face.

I would kill for a grown-up conversation.

Pippa surveyed the slightly messy house. Was she imagining it, or did lovely spacious Laurel Villa seem smaller than when they first moved there?

The walls are closing in.

Pippa moved decisively. Changing bag, phone, purse, keys, book. She popped Ruby into the waiting pushchair. 'Come on, Freddie. We're going out.'

'Ohhhhhh... *SuperMouse* is on soon!'

'Freddie, *SuperMouse* is always on somewhere. The sun never sets on *SuperMouse*.'

Freddie's brow crinkled. 'No it isn't. It's on at 3.30. It says on the TV thing.'

'Never mind. We need food.' She wasn't sure they did, but it was a better reason than saying to your three year old that if you didn't exchange two words with a grown-up who wasn't your mother-in-law then you would explode.

'Can we go and see Auntie Marge?'

'Yes!' The black cloud lifted. 'Brilliant idea, Freddie!' Marge would make tea, and keep Freddie busy, and *not lecture her*.

'Yeehaa!' Freddie punched the air. Where had he learnt that? Still, he would learn a lot of new things at preschool. She would have to get used to it.

Pippa hummed as she manoeuvred the pushchair out of the porch. The up-and-down thing was probably just hormones. She was perfectly fine now. All she had needed was a change of scene.

CHAPTER 2

'Are we nearly there?' Freddie said, stomping beside the pushchair.

'Freddie, we left the house two minutes ago. Hold on to the pushchair, please, we're crossing over.' Pippa looked both ways, even though the road was quiet, to set a good example.

'I wish Auntie Marge still lived on our road,' Freddie grumbled.

'Well, she lives five minutes away now.'

'Five minutes!' Freddie's eyes were full of woe. 'That's miles and miles!'

Pippa bit her tongue to maintain her self-control, and they walked silently for at least thirty seconds, Freddie trailing behind with his lower lip thrust out.

His sulk vanished instantly as they reached the village green. 'Can we feed the ducks?'

'Maybe afterwards,' said Pippa.

'Promise?'

'OK.'

Freddie smiled up at her. Already she felt heaps better. 'Come on, Mummy!'

They wheeled alongside the green, past the war memorial, over the bridge, and down by the river, sparkling in the pale winter sun.

Freddie tugged on her sleeve. 'What if Auntie Marge is out?'

'Then we'll come another time.' She shivered despite the bright sunshine. *Please be in, Marge. Don't be busy.*

They turned into River Lane. 'Look!' Freddie stopped dead, bringing the pushchair up with a jerk.

Pippa dragged her eyes away from the door of Wisteria Cottage, and followed Freddie's pointing finger to their former cramped, dingy, and unloved home, Rosebud Cottage.

Pippa blinked. Was it the same house?

Rosebud Cottage had blossomed. The door was painted sky-blue, and a garland of willow studded with pink and white roses hung on it. The windows were decorated with strings of pink and white bunting. The picket fence was white, not rotten brown. The garden had been tamed. Sitting in it, on a tartan rug, was a perfectly-groomed Afghan hound. Next to the dog knelt a young woman, her dark hair skewered up with a chopstick, unloading a wicker picnic hamper.

Pippa wanted to cry all over again. 'Don't stare, Freddie,' she said, in an undertone. 'We're visiting Auntie Marge.'

'She's having a picnic with a dog!' blared Freddie.

The young woman turned, beamed, and waved. 'Hi!'

'Hello.' Pippa nodded, then shoved the pushchair forward, over the cobbles. 'You can knock on Auntie Marge's door, Freddie.'

'Yay!' Freddie galloped ahead and launched himself

into the air to try and reach the door knocker, slamming against the door. 'Helloooooo!' he shouted, rattling the letterbox.

'All right, all right!' Marge's voice seemed to be coming from a long way inside the house, and it sounded cross. 'Beyoncé, shift yourself.' A pause. 'Yes, you.' An angry yowl followed. Pippa began to regret coming.

The door jerked open and Marge peered out. 'Oh! It's you.' Her expression switched from annoyed to relieved. 'Come on in. Can you get that beast over the step, or will you leave it outside?' Beyoncé stood beside her, tail flicking.

'I'll park it.' Pippa put the brake on, lifted Ruby out, and nudged Freddie into the house.

'Hello, young man,' said Marge.

'Hello, Auntie Marge!' Freddie hugged as high as he could reach, which was Marge's waist, then bent to pat Beyoncé, who took it quite well. 'Can we have a picnic? *She* is.'

'She?' Marge raised an eyebrow, which was wasted on Freddie.

'At our old house. But it's a new house. Can we? Pleeease?'

'Ohhh.' Marge glanced at Pippa, who shook her head. 'We'll see. But I think your mum would like a brew and a sit down first. You can have squash and a cake. Then maybe we could go fishing in the river, as it isn't too cold. My grand-daughter's wellies'll fit you.'

'Yay-yay-yay!' shouted Freddie. 'We can catch fish an' eat it!'

'Now that's a plan,' said Marge, opening a drawer and pulling out a large notepad and a pencil. 'Can you draw me a picture of us catching a big fish?'

'Yeah!' Freddie opened the notepad randomly and set to work.

'That should give us at least five minutes,' murmured Marge, leading the way to her galley kitchen and switching on the kettle. 'How are you, Pippa?'

'I'm OK.' Pippa moved Ruby onto her shoulder.

Marge chuckled at Ruby's solemn stare. Then her smile faded as her gaze shifted to Pippa. 'I hope you don't mind me saying, but you look exhausted.'

'I'm fine. Ruby didn't sleep well last night, that's all.'

'Mm.' Marge slam-dunked teabags into two mugs. 'You need a break.'

'And how am I supposed to do that?' Pippa retorted. Ruby's little body stiffened. 'Sorry, Rubes. I didn't mean to shout.' She rubbed the baby's back. 'And sorry, Marge. I think I'm just a bit tense. Simon is helping, really he is, but he's working late a lot, with the merger —'

'And when the merger's merged there'll be something else. He's that kind of person. Focused.' The kettle pinged and Marge filled the mugs. 'I used to watch him scrumping my apples back in the day. Even then he wouldn't go for the first apple he could find. He went for the best ones. Drove me mad, it did. I'd have my eye on a lovely ripe apple, just out of reach, and boom, he'd snaffle it before it hit the ground. Blighter.' She cackled as she spooned the teabags out and flicked them into the bin. 'Anyway, we didn't come in here to reminisce about your husband's misspent youth. What about you?'

'What about me?' Pippa leaned on the worktop and gently disengaged Ruby's hand from her hair.

'When did you last do something for yourself?' Marge

sidestepped Pippa to get to the fridge. 'Go somewhere on your own?' She banged the fridge door shut. 'Simon's perfectly capable of minding the children, especially now madam is getting so big.'

I must have gone out alone at some point in the last three months... There had been playdates, and they had gone out for lunch, of course, and her parents had come down from the Highlands to see the baby, and Suze had visited for a weekend... She had arranged a girls' night out with Lila last month, but Bella had been poorly...

'Thought so,' said Marge, lifting Ruby away and indicating a steaming mug of tea. 'You need a hobby.'

'But what?'

'Anything really, so long as you can't take the kids and it happens somewhere else. Aerobics, Morris dancing, conversational Spanish, whatever.' Marge swayed Ruby from side to side, grinning. 'I used to take two evening classes a week while Mr Marge babysat. Tuesdays and Thursdays. Didn't care what they were. I wove baskets, learnt Esperanto, stripped down a car engine...' She waved a hand. 'Something different.'

Pippa blew on her tea. 'I'm not sure I have enough brain left to do anything like that.'

'Of course you have!' snapped Marge. 'You solved a crime, for heaven's sake, you just need time when you can call your brain your own. Wait here.' She stalked off, returning a moment later. 'I knew I'd kept this for a reason.' She put a small booklet into Pippa's hand.

Pippa eyed it. *Gadcester College: Evening Courses, 2017-8.* 'I don't know —'

'You don't have to decide now.' Marge gulped her tea and clanked the mug down. 'Take it with you, read it, pick a class. Or find something on the parish board. Ask Simon to support you in this once a week.' She gave Pippa a steely look. 'Or if he won't, I will.'

'Thanks, Marge,' said Pippa. Her stomach was doing little flips and she couldn't tell whether it was excitement or fear.

'Auntie Marge!' called Freddie. 'I drew a fish!' He ran in with the notepad.

'That's a whale!' Marge said, inspecting it. 'I think we'd need a harpoon to catch that.' She held the drawing up. Two stick figures posed with stick nets, and one (the smaller) was holding a fish twice its size.

'Can we try?' Freddie jumped up and down.

'Let your mum finish her tea first,' said Marge. 'I'll sort the nets out, if you'll have Ruby back.'

'Of course I will.' Marge held Ruby out and she stretched fat little hands towards Pippa, who could have wept with love. Ruby nestled close, and for a second Pippa wondered how she could ever leave her baby with someone else and go out into the big world on her own. But Marge gave her a stern look, and Pippa reflected that one day Ruby would be a toddler, then a preschooler, and, at an unthinkable point in the future, older than Freddie was now.

'Fiiiiiiiish!' Marge opened the front door for Freddie, who charged down the lane to the river, brandishing his net. Marge followed, skirt tucked up and net in hand, and Pippa brought up the rear with Ruby.

The picnic was still in progress at Rosebud Cottage . . . or was it? The Afghan hound was sitting on the rug, showing incredible self-control as a cupcake — was it topped with dog treats? — was placed before it. On the side of the rug was a stand of finger sandwiches and scones, with dishes of jam and clotted cream. The woman laid out plates, cutlery and napkins. 'Staaaaayyy, Monty,' she said to the hound. Then she scurried backwards, taking pictures on her phone. 'Good boy!' she said at last to the dog, who barked, once, and gave him the cupcake. As he ate, she turned round, picked up the cake stand, and took several selfies of herself. She was slight, pretty, and looked about fifteen.

Pippa tiptoed past, feeling as if she was trespassing on a film set, and joined Marge and Freddie at the river.

'Who's your new neighbour?' she muttered.

Marge made a couple of passes with her net before answering. 'She moved in last month. I'm not sure what she said to the landlord, or the estate agents, but there've been more workmen in and out than I've had hot dinners. And her filming it. She did introduce herself. An odd sort of name. She said she was . . . a vogga. Whatever that is. Never vogged, myself.'

'A vlogger?' Pippa shaded her eyes and peered back to the garden of Rosebud Cottage, where the woman was walking up the garden path with the cake stand.

'That's it. Her phone's surgically attached to her hand. Although I must say the dog is very well-behaved. He could teach Beyoncé a thing or two. Or maybe it's the other way round.' Marge twisted her net and inspected the contents. 'Pah.' She dipped it again. 'So what does a valogger do?'

'Ask a teenager.' Pippa watched Freddie jab at the riverbed. 'To my limited knowledge, they put videos on YouTube, and have channels.'

'Ohhh, social media,' said Marge, dismissively. 'I

suppose she has followers and all that.'

'Probably,' said Pippa.

'Come here, little fishies!' shouted Freddie.

'Excuse me,' said a tinkly, Londonish voice behind them. Pippa whipped round, hoping they hadn't been overheard. But the woman was smiling. 'Would you mind if I took a picture of your little boy fishing? He's very cute.'

'Die, fishies, die!' Freddie yelled.

'Erm, what are you planning to do with it?' asked Pippa. She hoped she didn't sound too rude, but having worked in PR, she figured it was best to get things straight.

'Oh, no!' Her laugh was like silver bells. 'I wouldn't use it for anything without your permission. I just thought he was sweet. I won't if you'd rather I didn't.' She backed away a little, and her eyes were huge and green in her heart-shaped face.

Now Pippa felt mean. 'I don't mind. You can take a picture, so long as you don't put it online. Oh, and you send me a copy.'

'Of course!' She stepped forward and held the phone out, photographing Freddie as he fished. 'What's your email? I'll send you the photos once I've edited them. I'd Bluetooth them, but I don't think that works here.'

'It doesn't,' said Pippa. 'I'll write it down.' Pippa fished in her bag for pen and paper. 'Could you hold Ruby for a second, Marge?' Marge obliged, and Pippa scribbled her email address on a napkin.

The woman looked at it and whistled. 'You're Pippa Parker, the murder lady! I read about you online!'

'Oh God,' said Pippa. 'Which paper?'

'Dunno.' She studied Pippa more closely. 'You're in

great shape.'

'That'll be the *Gadcester Chronicle* then,' said Pippa. 'I'm twenty-nine. It was a misprint.'

'Ohhh.' She turned her head at a whine from up the lane. 'Sounds like my time's up. It was nice to meet you. I'll mail the pics.'

'Thanks, I'll keep an eye out for them,' called Pippa. 'What's your name?'

The answer floated back and Pippa looked at Marge. 'Did I mishear that?'

'Nope. I knew it was weird,' said Marge. 'Serendipity Jones.'

CHAPTER 3

Pippa hit *Pause* on her phone, lay back on the sofa, and sighed. Miracle of miracles, the children were both asleep and the house was quiet. But she felt ill from bingeing on Serendipity Jones's online presence, as if she had eaten too many over-iced cupcakes.

She had Googled Serendipity as soon as the children were in bed, watching craft videos guiltily with the volume turned down. Serendipity had her own YouTube channel, where she decoupaged and bunted and appliquéd — and baked, of course. A weblink led to her pastel-coloured blog, where Serendipity leaned on the windowsill of Rosebud Cottage and smiled at the world. Monty also featured, immaculately groomed and wearing a red bandana. Pippa wondered if Serendipity spent all her time crafting and brushing her dog, and what she was doing here, in Much Gadding.

Pippa's eye fell on the evening classes booklet which Marge had given her. She opened it at random. *Appreciating Poetry. Car Maintenance for Beginners. Intermediate Italian. Basic Bookkeeping.* She shuddered.

Ping! You have new mail. Pippa touched the screen.

It was from Serendipity.

Hi! Here's the best photo — the rest were blurred. I can send them if you like but the files are big. Best, S. Underneath was her email signature, formatted as a sugar-pink business card with swirly mauve script. *Serendipity Jones, Lifestyle Blogger and Crafter at Large.* Beneath was a battery of links. Pippa's fingers itched to click them and do a bit more snooping; but there was a paperclip to be investigated first. Her thumb hovered, and came down.

There was Freddie, standing in the river, trousers rolled, grinning as he lifted his net into the air. A spray of droplets arced on his left-hand side, and he was perfectly lit by the afternoon sun. When had her little boy become so beautiful?

She wiped her eyes hastily at the scrape of Simon's key in the door. 'Sorry, Pip, my meeting overran. I meant to text but then we got into a discussion about delayering —' His voice tailed off as he came into the sitting room and saw her. 'Are you all right?'

'I'm fine,' Pippa choked. 'It's just —' She held up the phone to show him Freddie.

Simon grinned. 'Aww, that's really nice. Did you take it?'

'Noooooo…' Her chest was swelling with sobs, and she had absolutely no control over it at all.

Simon sat down and put his arms awkwardly round her. 'Why are you upset?' he asked, softly. 'Did you have a bad day?'

'It was the same as every other day!' she wailed. 'Why can't *I* take great photos and make cupcakes?'

She could feel him drawing back slightly. 'Is that what you want to do?'

'No!' She felt in her sleeve for a tissue and blew her nose. 'I want to do . . . something that I want to do.'

'Oh.' He squeezed her gently, then picked up the evening class booklet.

'Nothing in there,' she said, and he dropped it on the sofa.

'Then what?' He eyed her as if she were an unexploded bomb. 'Are you sure you're all right?'

'Yes. I'm fine. I — I just think I need some time away from the kids. Once a week or so,' she added hastily.

'Oh. OK. You could have said, you know.'

'I know. But I didn't know that — that was what it was.'

'I'm sorry.' He pulled Pippa to him and kissed the top of her head. 'So if you're not going to learn Spanish or make wedding cakes, what do you have in mind?'

'I'm not sure.' Pippa cast her mind back to the paper flapping on the parish board. What groups were there in Much Gadding?

'You could meet people at the WI, and Mum says they have all sorts of different speakers —'

Pippa shook her head, afraid that if she opened her mouth she would insult either Sheila, the WI, or both, and then be pelted with rock cakes and evicted from the village.

'What about bridge?'

'Too complicated.'

'Nonsense, Mum manages perfectly well.'

Good grief, could he only think of his mum's hobbies?

'Maybe if you tried the evening classes, Mum could come with you. So you wouldn't be on your own.'

Pippa tried not to recoil. 'Um, no, there was something on the noticeboard, now what was it…'

Her mind groped desperately for something that wouldn't tempt Sheila, that she couldn't be persuaded into joining. A memory of Ruby bawling came to her, and of Sheila getting up from the Moses basket looking perplexed, saying 'I was only singing her a lullaby…'

'Choir!' she exclaimed. 'I'll join a choir. Singing's uplifting, it'll do me good.'

'A choir,' Simon repeated, his face neutral. 'Like a church choir?'

'Nooo!' Although she had sort of been thinking of a gospel choir, a jolly kind of Oh Happy Day outfit… 'More like… More like *Pitch Perfect*! Harmonies and stuff.'

'I've only ever heard you sing in the shower. Oh, and in church.' Simon loosened his tie. 'Wait a minute, I think I've seen *Pitch Perfect*. Wasn't there vomiting?'

'The choir I join won't do vomiting,' Pippa declared.

'And I'm sure there was sexy dancing at the end…'

'I can't promise that,' grinned Pippa.

'I think you should keep the sexy dancing for me.' Simon flung his tie over the back of the sofa. 'It's nice to see you smiling.' He ruffled Pippa's hair, gently, then kissed the side of her neck.

'Is Daddy home?' called a little voice from upstairs.

'Aargh,' Simon said into her shoulder. 'Hello, Freddie,' he called. 'I'll come and tuck you in, but then you have to go to sleep.'

'Yes, Daddy,' Freddie said, with the voice of an angel.

'Back in a minute,' Simon said, retrieving his tie.

'Help me up, would you.' Pippa stuck out her hand. 'I'd better go and sort dinner. I wasn't sure when you'd be back.'

'What is it?'

Pippa made a face. 'Chicken ping with pasta.'

'Ah, it'll do.' Simon took the stairs two at a time. Pippa watched him to the landing, then went into the kitchen, took a large ready meal from the fridge, and stabbed it viciously with a fork.

As the microwave hummed she searched for *choir Much Gadding* on her phone. She had never heard of a local choir, but then again she had never gone looking for one before. At the top of the search results was Sweet Harmony, followed by Short Back and Sides, and then a series of results relating to chairs.

Pippa read the descriptions for both. Sweet Harmony claimed to be 'a community choir singing a variety of music,' while Short Back and Sides advertised themselves as 'shoot-from-the-hip songsters who are never off-key'. Plus from the photo, they were men-only.

Sweet Harmony it was, then. She clicked on the link. *Fortnightly meetings on Wednesdays, 7.30-9.30pm, Lower Gadding, St Columba's Church Hall. No auditions.*

Kerching! Sold!

Ping! She opened the microwave door, retrieved the steaming plastic tray, and stirred the contents before sliding the meal back in and resetting the timer.

'Thank heavens for microwaves,' said Simon, padding into the kitchen in his socks and retrieving a bottle of beer from the fridge.

'How are alternate Wednesdays for you?'

He opened the bottle and took a swig. 'I generally find they happen in the middle of every other week.'

'You know what I mean.'

'Is it choir stuff?'

'Could be.' Pippa took a deep breath. 'Yes. Yes, it is.'

Simon shrugged. 'They're fine. Unless there's some sort of work emergency.'

'Ah yes, a widget crisis.' Pippa fetched plates and cutlery and put them on the worktop.

'Could happen. I remember the Great Widget Disaster of 2013 —'

'Oh, stop it.' The microwave pinged for the final time and Pippa turned the creamy strands onto the plates. 'Here you go.'

'Thanks.' They sat at one end of the dining table, half-facing each other. 'Want some?' Simon tilted the beer bottle towards Pippa.

'I'd love some, but better not. I don't think Ruby's ready to mix beer and milk yet.'

'Euww.' Simon drank some more, then twirled pasta round his fork. 'So who took the photo?'

'The photo? Oh.' That seemed hours ago. 'Someone I met today. She's taken on Rosebud Cottage. Serendipity Jones.' Simon raised his eyebrows. 'She's a vlogger-blogger,' Pippa said, in explanation.

'Well, maybe she should be a phogger. It's a great picture, we could put it on the wall.'

'Yeah. I'll tell her.' Pippa chased a mushroom round her plate.

'So is it just her in the cottage?'

'Nope. She's got an Afghan hound.'

'Wooow.'

'I know. But you wouldn't recognise the house. It looks like a trendy beach hut. In a good way.' Pippa sighed.

Simon's eyes narrowed. 'Did she make you feel inadequate?'

'No!' Pippa set her fork down harder than she had

meant. 'Maybe a bit,' she admitted. 'I don't think she meant to. She seemed nice.'

'OK.' Simon ruminated, and swallowed. 'Could-be-a-friend nice?'

'Not sure.' Pippa stretched across the table and sipped Simon's beer. 'How was Freddie when you went up?'

'Fine. Sleepy.'

'Good.'

They sat for a while, comfortably silent, before Pippa got up to clear the plates. 'So when does this choir of yours start?'

'There's a rehearsal next Wednesday. That's good, I might need a distraction.' Simon looked blank. 'It's Freddie's first session at preschool that morning.'

'Ohhhh. That's come round quickly.'

'It has.' Pippa went into the kitchen and put the plates into the dishwasher, then came back and leaned on the doorframe. 'He's ready. I'm not sure I am.'

'Do you want to talk about it?'

Pippa considered. 'Honestly? What I really want to do right now is flop on the sofa and watch mindless rubbish on the TV with you until Ruby's next feed.'

'You old romantic.' Simon put an arm round her. He was warm under his work shirt, but she just didn't have the energy. 'Come on then.' And he escorted her into the lounge, scooping up the remote on the way to the sofa.

CHAPTER 4

'What are you doing?' Simon mumbled into the pillow. 'I didn't hear Ruby.'

'I'm going for a jog.' Pippa tied the cord of her tracksuit bottoms.

'What?' Simon rolled over and stared at her. 'The sun isn't even up yet — *I'm* not even up yet!' He fumbled for his watch.

'Exactly.' Pippa opened the wardrobe and shook out a sweatshirt. Her next words were slightly muffled. 'I'm just off for a little jog round the village.' Her head popped out from the fleece. 'Ruby doesn't usually wake up till after seven, and there's a bottle of milk in the fridge. I won't be more than twenty minutes.' In truth, she doubted she'd manage to jog for more than five; but she could always walk the rest.

'What's brought this on?'

'Nothing. Be back soon.'

Pippa tiptoed downstairs, laced up her trainers, and grabbed the small set of keys from the hall table. She could carry her phone. She steeled herself for a piping 'Mummy?' from upstairs, but it never came.

The porch was considerably cooler than the hall, and she closed the inner door quickly before unlocking the front door.

Wow, it's cold. Still, that would make her go faster. Pippa set off at a fast walk, arms pumping, wishing she'd worn a hat. The only hat she owned, though, was a large cream cable-knit bobble hat, which seemed somehow incompatible with fitness.

Pippa power-walked down the street and turned left. Once she'd warmed up, she would jog into the village, past the green, up Lila's road, round the corner to Imogen's, back to the green, then home. Nice safe roads that she knew in the grey pre-dawn. If she was feeling diligent, she might even do two laps.

The roads were quiet. Some houses had lights on and Pippa thought of the people inside; gliding about in dressing-gowns, putting the kettle on, feeding the toaster with bread, adjusting the temperature in the shower. It took her mind off how strange it was to be out, alone, at this time of day.

A fluorescent-yellow shape was heading her way. A runner, plugged into his headphones, staring straight ahead, face blank. Pippa moved out of his way, then turned to watch. His legs moved with the regularity of pistons. She exhaled, her breath making a cloud in front of her, and broke into a slow jog.

What had brought this on?

Serendipity Jones, probably. She had the figure of someone who had never had children. Probably because she had time to do yoga and walk her dog. Pippa rapped herself over the mental knuckles. It was willpower and discipline. Those sort of excuses were padding her squishy tummy and wobbly thighs, even three months on. This was despite her New Year's Resolution to get fit, which had vanished from her memory with the Christmas chocolates. She gritted her teeth and jogged a little faster. When she went to choir practice, she would not have the get-out clause of Ruby, her protective, cuddly shield. She would have to stand alone.

And there was something else. Large, looming, not terrifying exactly, but unwelcome.

Her thirtieth birthday. It was coming in a few weeks, creeping up on her with a net like Freddie's.

She had already told Simon that she didn't want a fuss. 'A nice meal in the village, just you and me. If you organise a do where people jump out at me yelling "Surprise!", I will kill you.'

'Thanks for the heads-up,' he had said, off-handedly. She was almost sure that he wasn't up to anything he shouldn't be.

But you like parties. She slogged towards the green, dark except for small pools of light from the wrought-iron street lamps.

But I don't want to be thirty. And the support underwear I'd have to buy to fit into a cocktail dress...

A car swished by on the other side of the green. Pippa looked at her watch. Had she really only been doing this for three minutes? It felt as if she had been exercising for ever. That showed how unfit she was. She was not just warmed up, but roasting, and sweat was trickling down her back.

She had never noticed before that Lila's road was slightly uphill. It was actually quite a gradient when you ran it. Pippa puffed her way along. At least Lila wouldn't be up. If she were, she'd probably shout something rude. In a friendly way, of course. Pippa automatically glanced at Lila's house, and nearly fell over her own feet. The door was open, and a stream of light spilled out, illuminating a big-haired shape leaning into a car with its engine running.

Pippa shot across the road, her breath coming in ragged gasps, and feeling warmer than ever. Lila giggled, and Pippa heard murmuring, but the noise of the car made it hard to make out what was said. Pippa ran past. Her heart felt as if it would jump out of her chest, but she couldn't stop. The thought of being seen made her want to die. Not just because she was convinced she was a hot mess, but Lila would know that she had been spotted.

The car drove away, and seconds later a door closed. Only then did Pippa slow to a walk. Her face burned, and blood sang in her ears. 'I think that's enough for a first time,' she said to herself. She did not allow herself to think any more until she had turned off Lila's street.

Pippa tried to formulate more than one explanation for Lila leaning into a car at this time of the morning, but it was pointless. She was saying goodbye to someone, and that laugh suggested it was someone who had spent the night there.

Which was fine. Of course it was. *Lila's activities are none of my business.*

But why hadn't Lila mentioned anyone?

Was it a one-night stand?

Impossible. Lila would never do that with Bella in the house. Pippa's mind flashed back to Lila at playgroup, smiling to herself as she texted.

Lila's seeing someone. Why don't I know about it?

Sudden indignation prickled her into bursting into a run

again, but the feeling only boosted her for a few steps before the cold air made her cough and slow down. *Fine. I'll power walk. That's just as good.* Pippa pumped her arms and strode out, puffing dragon breath into the air.

Who's Lila seeing, and why hasn't she told me?

The obvious answer was that it was someone completely unsuitable.

Much younger? On drugs?
Married?

Pippa shook her head to clear it. She was back at the green, anyway, and could take the short side this time. Her watch revealed that she had been out for nearly nine minutes. *God, this fitness thing is hard work.* What did Serendipity Jones do? She imagined her in pastel workout gear in a dance studio, dipping into an arabesque. *Gah.*

It seemed much quicker to get home. Simon, still in his dressing-gown, was pouring himself a coffee. 'How was it?'

'Hard.' Pippa got herself a glass of water, gulped it down and refilled it.

'Well, you got out and did it. Good for you.'

'Any noise from upstairs?'

'Nothing.'

'Good.' Pippa ran a hand through her sweaty hair. 'I'll get a quick shower.'

Five minutes later, feeling considerably more human, she tied her dressing-gown cord and walked downstairs. 'Toast?' She put two slices in for herself and got the jam out of the fridge.

Simon looked pointedly at the jar. Pippa stuck her tongue out at him, then sighed and put it back. 'It's so not fair.'

'I know. One slice for me, please. I'll take fruit in.'

'Now you're showboating.' Pippa dropped another piece of bread in and pushed the levers down.

'Will you be doing this regularly?' Simon sipped from his mug.

Pippa thought it over. 'I probably should,' she admitted.

'In that case, maybe get some running shoes.'

The baby alarm crackled, then rustled. Ruby whimpered at high volume.

'Here we go,' muttered Pippa, making for the stairs.

By the time Simon came back upstairs, plate of toast in hand, Ruby was settled in for her morning feed, sucking away contentedly. Pippa remembered the metronome-like legs of the passing runner, and a Friesian cow lumbered into her mind.

'Someone's peckish.' Simon put the plate on the bedside table.

'Thanks.' Pippa glanced at the bobbing head. 'The way she's feeding at the moment, I ought to be a size ten.'

'You're lovely as you are.' Pippa looked up, startled. Simon was gazing at her, a soft smile on his face.

'I'd give you a hug, but — well —' Her eyes flicked down to Ruby. 'Thanks.'

'S'fine.' He went into the bathroom. Water hissed from the shower.

Pippa let her mind drift as Ruby chomped on. She could just do with a little snooze… She let her head fall back, and winced as it met the headboard. Ruby jumped, and Pippa stroked her head until she settled.

How can I find out who Lila's seeing?

I'm not being nosy, exactly. It's in her best interests.

Would Imogen know? After all, she lived round the

corner. Pippa reached for her phone and scrolled through her messages, then glanced at the sliver of dark sky at the window and dropped the phone on the bed. Later, maybe, she could suggest a playdate, or coffee. Freddie would love a surprise visit to his friend Henry. 'Come on, Ruby,' she said, shifting a little on the bed.

Ruby lifted her head and gazed at Pippa with huge blue eyes. 'Don't look at me like that,' said Pippa, stroking her cheek. 'I suppose you want the other side.' She turned Ruby round and sighed an 'aaaah' of pleasure as Ruby got to work and the pressure lessened. Inconvenient it might be, and sometimes uncomfortable, but she would miss feeding Ruby herself when the time came. Serendipity Jones would probably look like some sort of madonna —

Stop thinking about that woman! She was beginning to irritate herself, even. Pippa's fingers itched to text Imogen, but she settled the matter by throwing the phone further down the bed, out of reach. *From today, Pippa Parker*, she told herself, *you are a woman with willpower. Starting now.*

CHAPTER 5

'He'll be absolutely fine,' Mrs Marks said, again. 'Won't you, Freddie?'

Freddie didn't look convinced.

'There we are,' she said, comfortably, leaning down slightly and holding out a hand. Freddie, to his credit, stepped forward and took it instead of cowering behind Pippa.

'Could I stay for a little while?' Pippa peered through the squared safety-glass window at the other children, who were sitting in a circle on the rug.

Mrs Marks blinked. 'I understand the first time is hard, but we recommend that parents don't stay. It makes the children harder to settle, because they keep looking for you.' She smiled. 'If Freddie really isn't enjoying it, we can always contact you. If you're available.'

'I'm available,' said Pippa, firmly. 'Do you need my mob —'

'We've got it.' Mrs Marks opened the door and backed through it. 'Wave bye-bye, Freddie.' Freddie waved with the air of a condemned man, and the door clicked shut behind them.

'Just you and me then, Rubes.' Pippa wheeled the pram down the shallow step, rather at a loss. It was ten o'clock. Preschool would finish at half past twelve, assuming Freddie stayed the course. Mrs Marks had outlined a formable programme of activities, including story time, snacks, crafts, music time, and lunch, which made Pippa feel even more inept than usual.

But would Freddie enjoy it? Pippa imagined him standing in the middle of the room, looking at the door, slow tears running down his cheeks. She put the brake on the pushchair and walked down the path. She peered through the window. Where was Freddie? Then her eyes met Mrs Marks's, and she scuttled away.

Pippa had reached the school gate when she stopped abruptly. *It's perfectly normal to check that my child is all right!* She executed a three-point turn and marched back up the path. But she couldn't approach that door again.

Hmm. Pippa parked Ruby on the grass and walked round the side of the wooden building. There was a small window, high up, and someone had left a metal pail, upside down. This was obviously the local parents' checkpoint. Pippa moved the bucket a little closer to the wall, put a foot on it, and stepped up, gripping the window-ledge with both hands.

Cautiously, she raised her head until she could see in. Everyone seemed busy. Good. She scanned the room for a little figure in a *SuperMouse* T-shirt (he had insisted). She couldn't see any children by themselves, which was good. Unless he was crying in the toilet —

Laughter wafted through the glass and then she saw Freddie, giggling helplessly, sitting between two children she didn't know. Some hands shot up, Freddie's among them. He spoke, then beamed as everyone clapped.

Pippa stepped off the bucket and wheeled Ruby away. *You should be happy that he's happy*, she scolded herself.

All that worrying, all those what-ifs, and he was absolutely fine.

Pippa was at her own front door before she realised it. She changed Ruby and put her down for a nap, then made herself a cup of tea and stared into space.

She had no excuse not to be putting a wash on, or cleaning the kitchen floor, or any amount of domestic chores.

Pippa went into the sitting room and picked her book up from the side table. But she didn't want to read, either.

Her phone buzzed. A text, from Simon. *How did it go?*

Fine, she replied.

Oh good x.

Pippa put the book down, and her phone on top of it, and walked to the window. Freddie was probably having a snack, eating carrot sticks, or an apple. Something he wouldn't touch at home. Her nose wrinkled.

Perhaps this was normal, this feeling of being abandoned by your own child. Lila would tell —

She probably would, but texting wasn't an option. Lila would suggest coffee, and either she would say yes and end up blurting out what she'd seen, or she'd have to invent an excuse, and that would be a lie.

Why was everything so complicated?

Maybe a walk would help. Exercise was supposed to de-stress you, wasn't it?

Ruby was blinking but not asleep yet. Pippa scooped her up and Ruby squeaked. 'I know,' said Pippa, soothing her. 'Mummy's all over the place.'

How could she find out what was going on with Lila? Imogen had responded to her coffee text on Friday with *Sorry in Spain. Didn't I say?*

Imogen probably had, and she'd completely missed it. *One more thing to beat myself up about.*

Pippa inserted Ruby into her snowsuit, and mobilised the pushchair. A nice, long walk would help. It had better.

The pond on the village green was still frozen, and the ducks were sliding all over the place. Pippa lifted Ruby out and sat on the bench. 'Look, Ruby! Skating ducks!'

'Hello.'

Pippa looked up. It was Sam.

It would be.

Sam sat beside her. 'Livvy's at preschool,' she explained.

'So's Freddie.' Pippa fought with her urge not to say any more, and won. 'It's his first day today.'

'Oh dear.' Sam's voice oozed sympathy, but there was a gleam in her eye that Pippa couldn't interpret. 'Was he all right?'

'He seemed fine,' Pippa said, quietly.

'Livvy hated it at first,' Sam confided. 'She used to hang on to my leg and cry. I had to promise I'd come back in ten minutes. It took months before she could bear to be left for a full session.'

'Mmm. Look, Ruby, there's a squirrel.'

'But it's great that Freddie's so confident, away from you.' Sam paused, as if to let the hit sink in. 'Have you seen much of Lila lately?'

'Just the usual.' Sam was wearing a pleased, curious expression which Pippa found eminently slappable.

'Ohh. I wondered what you thought of her new man?'

'I haven't met him yet,' Pippa admitted unwillingly.

'Really? Hasn't Lila told you all about him?' Sam sniggered.

'I take it you've been introduced, Sam.'

'I don't think anyone's met him. Lila wants to keep him all to herself. But I saw them in the corner of the Fiddler, all cosied up.' Sam laughed again, and Pippa's fingers twitched. 'You should disguise yourself and go on the hunt for them, Pippa. It would be a shame to let your detective skills go to waste.' She stood up. 'Time for me to go. Livvy was upset when I left her this morning, so I'll fetch her early. Must be great to forget your kid for a couple of hours.' She strolled off, humming to herself.

Pippa unclenched her fists and got up, strapping Ruby into her pram. *So much for the de-stressing effect of a walk. My blood pressure's probably through the roof.* She checked her watch. *Is it really only ten past eleven?*

'Do you need anything, Ruby?' she asked.

No response; but then she hadn't expected one. Ruby just looked sleepy.

'Let's go home, then. Yes.' *I'm turning into one of those people who talk to themselves and pretend they're addressing the cat.*

***

'Yes, Freddie was ever so good,' said Mrs Marks, glancing over her shoulder at Freddie demolishing a biscuit. 'He played nicely, and shared, and ate everything up.'

Was Mrs Marks thinking of another child? This paragon didn't sound much like Freddie.

'Oh yes, and he painted a picture for you. He said you'd put it on the fridge.'

'Of course I will!' Pippa smiled.

'I'll go and get it.' Mrs Marks unpeeled herself from the door. 'Freddie! Your mum's here!'

'Do I have to?' whined Freddie.

'You can come back on — when's he in next?'

'Monday,' said Pippa, flatly.

'There, Monday.' Mrs Marks lifted up a large sheet of burnt-orange paper, adorned with slashes of blue and black paint at random intervals. 'Here you are, Mrs Parker. I think it's almost dry.' She handed Pippa two corners.

'Could you hold it for me, Freddie? I need to wheel Ruby.'

'But it's for you, Mummy! You have to hold it!'

'Fine.' Pippa doubled the paper over and clamped it between finger and thumb. 'Let's go, then.'

'Bye, everyone! Bye!' Freddie ran round the room on a sort of victory lap. 'How long till Monday?' he asked loudly, just before the door closed.

On the way home Freddie delivered a monologue on everything he had done that morning. 'And Mrs Marks read *The Gruffalo* — and we made all the noises — and we had rice cakes and grapes and cheese —'

'You ate rice cakes?'

'Yeah, they were nice.'

Pippa thought of the number of times she had cleared chunks of rice cake from under Freddie's chair, and said nothing.

'And we did painting, and sang songs and danced. Livvy's mum came to get her and she cried. Lots.'

'Ah,' said Pippa, storing the information for later.

'And we had big potato with beans and cheese and I ate it all. And Livvy's.'

'Wow, Freddie, you had a very good time at

preschool —'

'What are we doing this afternoon?'

'I'm not sure. But we'll definitely put your painting on the fridge.'

'Will we do ac-tiv-i-ties?' Freddie brought the word out proudly, like a large fossil.

'We'll see,' said Pippa. 'Come along, Freddie, some of us want our lunch.'

When she came to unfold Freddie's masterwork, paint had transferred itself to the other side of the paper. She put it up on the fridge while Freddie was in the toilet.

'Mummy!' he cried, as soon as he came in. 'My painting!'

'Sorry, Freddie, but next time you'll have to carry it home. Mummy doesn't have enough hands.'

Freddie stuck his lower lip out and stomped off, flinging himself on the sofa and staring moodily at the screen.

Pippa regarded the painting. It resembled a butterfly, or one of those things with the ink blots — Rorschach tests? She snorted. Given her current, slightly murderous state of mind, it was as well that no-one was likely to ask her what she thought Freddie's painting was supposed to be. The answer would probably get her locked up.

CHAPTER 6

Pippa hummed as she drove to Lower Gadding church hall. There was nothing to be worried about. She had been in the choir at school, and it would be nice to exercise her vocal cords somewhere other than the shower or the car. Besides, wasn't community singing meant to be uplifting? She imagined herself leaving the hall, cheeks glowing, full of enthusiasm for life and the world.

If she could park. The little patch of asphalt next to the hall was full already, and it was twenty past seven. Pippa circled, looking for somewhere to leave the Mini which wouldn't block either the road or someone's driveway, and ended up parking in a side street five minutes' walk away. By the time she reached the hall, she could hear noises like an orchestra warming up. *Wow, they're enthusiastic.* She put her hand on the doorknob, but something made her pause. What if she was meant to ring first, not just turn up? But there were no contact details on the webpage. Her stomach felt uneasy, though she had eaten early to avoid that very thing. *What if they don't want me?*

Pippa considered turning round and driving home, then imagined Simon's questions if she did. She could drive on to a pub, have a coffee, then go home. But Simon would winkle it out of her. He always did. The earnest conversations that would follow gave her the impetus to open the door.

A throng of people were gathering at the far end of the room. The conductor tapped her baton on the music stand. 'Come on, you lot!' They jostled good-humouredly into position. There must be thirty or forty of them. Had anyone seen her? Could she escape?

Someone must have caught the conductor's eye, for she turned, saw Pippa, and went to meet her, hand outstretched. She was slightly older than Pippa, perhaps thirty-five, with short dark hair. She was dressed in a black trouser suit and flats.

'Hello! I'm Jen,' she said, taking Pippa's hand and pumping it vigorously.

'Er, hello. I'm Pippa.'

'Welcome to Sweet Harmony, Pippa. Corny name, I know, but we are pretty harmonious. And friendly. Aren't we?'

'Yes!' the choir replied, not quite in unison.

'All right everyone, let's give Pippa a demonstration.' Jen flourished her baton. '"Help", please.' She blew on her pitch pipe, dropped into a conductor's crouch and the baton flicked up.

From the first complex chord to the last ooh, it was truly astonishing. The choir moved from pop through gospel, and the rap in the middle eight, delivered by a man with a grey mullet, was seamless. And they didn't just stand there and sing. Oh no. They also performed, gesturing in unison, sometimes singing to each other, sometimes addressing the audience of one.

The choir delivered the final note with all eyes on Pippa. 'So what do you think?' Jen asked.

Pippa eyed the choir, who were trying to look casual. 'It was — amazing,' she said at last, weakly. 'And very complicated.'

'Oh, you'll pick it up,' said Jen. 'Can you read music?'

Pippa nodded. Making a noise in front of these people suddenly seemed quite difficult.

'And can you keep time?'

'I think so.'

'There you are, that's all you need. Right everyone, the county heats are in three weeks and I'm still not happy with the headbanging section in "Bohemian Rhapsody". Let's go to it!' She turned to Pippa. 'Oh, wait.' She ran to a big leather case sitting on a chair at the side, and pulled out a music score, which she handed to Pippa. 'Join in when you're ready. Soprano or alto?'

'Alto,' murmured Pippa.

'OK, go next to Edie.' She pointed with her baton at a woman with short, white hair, dressed in jeans and a Hello Kitty jumper. 'Right! From Galileo, please.'

Being in the middle of the choir was like being buffeted by a storm. Noise came from all sides; the basses rumbled, the tenors hooted, the sopranos shrilled with the power and purity of car alarms.

By the time they stopped for a break, the choir had gone through 'Bohemian Rhapsody', 'Uptown Funk', and a drum and bass number — was it 'Freestyler'? Pippa's head was ringing. And so far, she hadn't sung a note.

Edie swigged on a bottle of water and indicated the biscuit tin sitting on the side table. 'Are you enjoying it?' she half-shouted. Pippa suspected her ears were ringing too.

'I'm finding it a bit hard to pick up,' Pippa said.

'What?'

'It's tricky,' Pippa shouted.

Edie laughed. 'When I first came I was too scared to open my mouth for weeks. One day I just thought, "Oh, what the hell," and gave it some welly. People come from miles around, you know.'

'Do they?' Pippa looked about her. Only one or two faces were familiar.

'Yes. We're not exclusive, unlike Short Back and Sides. They're a funny bunch,' said Edie, under her breath. 'They rehearse at the high school, in one of the soundproofed rooms. You'd think they were planning a robbery, not having a sing-song!' She laughed. 'Heaven knows what they'll bring out at the county heats.'

'What are the county heats?' asked Pippa, feeling completely clueless.

'Ooh, sorry. I forget that we speak our own language. Want a cuppa?' Edie led the way to a large urn, in front of which a ragged queue was forming. 'Have you heard of SingFest UK?'

'The national choir competition? Of course I have!'

'Well, there are heats and quarter-finals and semi-finals leading up to it, and what Jen mentioned is one. We have to perform a medley of three songs, and we haven't even practised the transitions here yet. Jen's got something pretty cool in mind, though, I can tell you. Tea or coffee?'

'Tea, please.' Edie obliged and handed her a styrofoam cup, then made herself a coffee, fishing in her jeans pocket and popping in a sweetener. 'Probably terrible for the voice, but I need the caffeine.'

'All right there, Edie?' The rapper wandered over, throwing his cup expertly into a bin on the way. 'Pippa, is it?' He peered at her. 'I think you're on my milk round.'

'Oh!' Pippa scrutinised him. 'I didn't recognise you without your overall.'

'Gerry's the name,' he said, extending a weatherbeaten hand. 'How are you finding it?'

'Honestly? It's a bit scary.'

'Don't worry, you don't have to join in till you're ready —'

'Places!' Jen strode past, clapping her hands, and the group followed her like rats following the Pied Piper. When everyone was assembled Jen tapped the stand. 'Now, some of you know what's going to happen next. Step forward if you do.'

Edie stepped forward smartly, as did Gerry, and two other people; a plump dark-haired woman and a tall, slightly stooped man in a golf sweater.

'Say hello to your soloists!' Jen picked up a sheaf of music from the floor, and gave a pile to each soloist. 'Now that we've got the basic songs down, I want to look at the transitions, and I've put something together. It's good on paper, but this is the world premiere.' Jen held up crossed fingers. Pippa heard rustling as the sheets were passed out, and also some muttering at the back. 'So, this is how it works. Listen up.' She began to deliver a lengthy explanation of the transition, which presumably made sense to most people there.

Pippa gave up and let her mind wander. As she did, her ears tuned into the muttering, which had resumed.

'It's always Edie...'

'Yeah, at least the sopranos take turns...'

'And the tenors…'

'Yeah. Thought the sopranos were meant to be the prima —'

'A-HEM!' Jen glared at a point behind Pippa. 'If we're quite ready, let's try the first transition.'

Pippa kept her mouth firmly shut as the choir attempted the first transition. It started well. Edie and the other four soloists came in at the final guitar solo, repeating it, gradually speeding it up. The choir followed.

But there was a dissonant voice. A few people behind her were staying on the original beat, and they weren't correcting themselves. They were getting louder. Other voices nearby were faltering, and joining the rebels, until the section was almost completely out of synch.

Jen made a cut motion with her hands, but some people were so preoccupied with trying to pick up their part that they didn't notice.

'Shut up!' she yelled.

The silence that followed was thick and accusing.

'Sorry to shout at you,' she said, putting her baton down. 'But what *was* that? Why weren't you watching me?'

There were murmurings, but no-one spoke up. Pippa longed to look round, but didn't dare move.

'We'll go again. Same place.' Jen raised the baton, but there was a crease between her brows, and she no longer stood so confidently.

And it happened again.

'Cut!' This time everyone obeyed. 'I don't know what the problem is, but if this happens on the day we can wave goodbye to any further participation in SingFest UK.' Jen gripped the music stand with both hands. 'I was going to suggest an optional rehearsal next Wednesday, but now it's compulsory.'

Whispering broke out, and Jen rapped the stand with her baton. 'Come on, folks. I don't like being heavy-handed but we can't present this. This was supposed to be the easy bit.' She slumped a little, then looked up. 'All right. I apologise that I didn't get these arrangements done before. I've been busy at work. Next time I won't leave it so late. We'll work on them next Wednesday, and if it really isn't happening then I'll think of something easier. Let's try it once more.' She raised the baton, and her hand, previously so steady, was quivering.

She cut the choir as soon as they began to diverge. 'That's enough. I think that some of you have a problem,' she said, staring at a point behind Pippa. 'I advise you to think things over before next Wednesday, and if you still have a problem, don't bother coming. That's it. I'm done. Go home.' Jen stepped back, her gaze steady, then gathered her music from the stand, folded it down, fetched her case, and left. The door banged, but didn't shut, and squeaked open. A minute later a car engine started.

No-one spoke until the noise of the car had faded. Then the murmurs resumed; but now they permeated the choir, and the buzz was rising. Edie looked furious, and the dark-haired soprano soloist was crying.

Pippa gazed around the room. Everyone was occupied. Small groups were forming, and probably discussing other groups, from the sidelong looks shooting here and there. *I don't need this.* She eased through the nearest two knots of people and went to get her bag.

'Wait!' Edie hurried over. 'We aren't usually like this. I'm sorry you had to see that. It's . . . complicated. Please don't think the worst of us.'

'It wasn't what I was expecting,' said Pippa.

'Put it down to pre-comp nerves,' said Edie. 'We'll be fine next week, just come back and see. Please.'

Pippa took her time driving off. No-one else left the hall in that time. *I hope they don't start a fight.* She drove home slowly, her window half-open to let the cold night air in. It was a relief after the torrid atmosphere in the hall.

'How was it?' Simon called softly from the sitting room.

Pippa dropped her keys on the hall table. 'Fraught.' The TV showed long shots of people looking overwrought, set to anguished strings. 'I think I could have stayed in and watched this. Same sort of experience, and I'd have saved the petrol.'

'I thought you were early.' Simon paused the TV and turned to her. 'What happened?'

'Discord. Of sound, and more.' Pippa sat in the small space left on the sofa. 'How were the kids?'

'Really good, actually.'

'Flaming typical.'

'Do you think you'll go back?' Simon's eyes were straying to the screen.

'You can put it on again if you want.' Simon clicked the remote, then moved his feet to give Pippa more room. 'I'll give it one more go, and if it doesn't improve, then —' She mimed cutting her throat.

'Not sweet harmony, then,' Simon said, looking straight ahead.

Pippa snorted. 'God, no.'

CHAPTER 7

'Can we go to the shops after playgroup?' Freddie fell into step beside Pippa as she wheeled Ruby down the road.

'Maybe. Why?'

Freddie looked sidelong at her. 'Can we get different beans?'

'Different beans?' Pippa stopped dead and stared at her son. 'But you love baked beans.'

Freddie traced circles on the pavement with his shoe, and muttered something. Pippa leaned down. 'What was that, Freddie?'

'Preschool beans are better. And the cheese is cheesier.'

'Is it.' Pippa walked on, then stopped when she realised that Freddie wasn't following.

'Can we?' he repeated, looking very small and steadfast.

'We'll see. Come on, Freddie, or we'll be late. It's our turn to put the toys out.' Freddie stood a moment longer, then ran to her, putting his hand on the pushchair handle. If only he was always so easy to win round.

Please be harmonious, Pippa thought, pushing Ruby down the concrete path to St Saviour's church hall. *After yesterday, I'm not sure I can take any more backbiting.*

She pulled the large iron key from her pocket. Even now, she felt a little frisson whenever she pushed open the door. Even though the murder — manslaughter, as the court had judged it to be — hadn't come to light in that way at all.

'Now then, Freddie, how many toys can we fetch from the cupboard before Ruby starts fussing?'

'Like a game?' asked Freddie, running to the toy cupboard.

'Exactly.' Pippa followed more sedately.

Ruby gave them three minutes before bursting into a wail. Pippa saw the pram starting to jerk. She released Ruby and popped her on the play mat, surrounded by a few things to rattle and bang.

The other parents straggled in, kids in tow. Caitlin had brought a tray of muffins. 'I'm not on drinks, am I?' she asked. 'I couldn't remember.' She touched her stomach, which was a little larger than the last time Pippa had seen her.

'No, I think it's Eva today. It'll be on the wall, anyway.'

'Yeah. I'll take these through to the kitchen.' But Caitlin lingered, moving a chair into place.

'I'll come too,' said Pippa. 'I need to check the urn, anyway.'

'Are you all right?' she asked, as they walked along the short corridor to the kitchen.

'Fine, fine. You go first.' Caitlin hung back. Pippa gave her a look, and pushed the kitchen door open.

And everything was normal.

'Here we are.' Pippa found the plastic door wedge and

kicked it into place. 'Is everything going well?'

'Oh yes.' Caitlin put her tray on the worktop. 'I'll put these out properly at break. I'll leave the tea towel on so they don't get stale.' She gazed round the kitchen as if casing the joint. 'I'll go and see what Dylan's doing.' Her footsteps pattered on the lino.

Pippa filled the jug with water and poured it into the urn. She'd learnt to bite her tongue when people behaved as if there was a corpse in every cupboard. Surely that was a once-in-a-lifetime thing. She retrieved the tray of cups and saucers and set it next to the muffins. There. Eva could do the rest.

The hall was much busier when she returned. Ruby was banging a rattle on the floor, squeaking and rolling like a pig in mud. Freddie and Dylan had commandeered the garage, and were doing ramp races. She looked for an empty chair. Only one was free...

Next to Lila, who was texting.

For a moment Pippa considered putting more chairs out. But then she told herself she was being ridiculous, and crossed the floor to her friend.

'Hi.'

Lila looked up. 'Oh, hi Pip.' She patted the chair seat, but her eyes slid back to her phone.

'Work stuff?' asked Pippa, sitting down.

Lila's phone beeped, and she snorted. 'Just . . . stuff.'

'Oh, OK.' Lila was dressed for work, which was normal for a Thursday, but there was something different about her. A sort of *glow* —

'Hello again, Pippa.' Sam had materialised from nowhere, little Livvy clinging to her hand.

'Hi, Sam.' Pippa tried to catch Lila's eye, to spark up a

conversation which would signal that she was busy. But Lila was completely absorbed in her phone.

'I wanted to let you know . . . when I went to pick up Livvy yesterday, Freddie had settled in really well. He was playing so nicely with the other children. Is he here today?' Sam scanned the room, as did Pippa. But wonder of wonders, Freddie was sitting with Dylan, turning over the pages of a picture book. 'I still can't get Livvy to let go of me for more than a few minutes at a time. Can I, honey?' She smiled at her daughter. 'You're so lucky.'

'Aw, every child is different,' said Pippa, feeling guilty. *I shouldn't think the worst of people, even if I don't like them.*

'Yes. You're absolutely right.' Sam beamed at her. 'Nice to have them off your hands, isn't it? Gives you more time to get on with your — *other activities.*' She gave Pippa a very significant look.

'Did I miss something?' said Lila, glancing up from her phone.

'Oh no, no, nothing at all,' said Sam, grinning and stepping back. 'I'll leave you to your investigations, Pippa. Good luck!' Sam led her daughter away through the litter of toys on the mat. She ought to have been felled stone dead by the look which Pippa threw at her departing back, but it slid harmlessly off, like a fried egg from a pan on TV.

'What was she talking about?' Lila frowned at Pippa, her phone now ignored in her lap.

'I don't know,' said Pippa, but she could feel heat creeping up her neck.

'Yes you do, you look guilty as hell. What are you up to?' Lila shifted round so that she was squared up to Pippa, and glared.

'You're very quick to assume it's about you,' Pippa found herself saying.

'Well, isn't it?' Lila's phone beeped, but she was too busy staring Pippa down to look.

'Maybe Sam's also noticed that you're glued to that phone lately. I can't remember the last time we had a proper conversation.' Pippa shrugged. 'It doesn't take a genius to work it out.'

'My life's my own business, and I'll see whoever I want,' Lila said, emphatically.

'Fine, but why the secrecy?'

'Why do you need to know?' Lila's voice was rising, and Pippa sensed that people were looking in their direction. 'Keep your nose out, Pippa. I'll tell you when I'm ready, not before. *If* I choose to.' Lila flounced across the room and flung herself into a chair set slightly apart. She resumed texting, glaring in Pippa's direction every so often.

Pippa considered leaving. She considered scooping Ruby up and dragging Freddie with her. But that would be letting Sam win, and also admitting she was in the wrong. OK, maybe she shouldn't have got drawn into the conversation in the first place... She sighed. Maybe she was slightly in the wrong. She got up and walked over to Lila, slumped in her chair, eyes fixed on her phone screen.

'Lila,' She had to say it twice before Lila looked up. 'I'd like a word. In the kitchen.'

Lila stared up at her. 'And what if I don't want a word?'

Pippa pursed her mouth up to keep from swearing in front of impressionable toddlers, until she was calm enough to speak. 'It's up to you. I'll be in the kitchen.'

Pippa took the opportunity to switch the urn on. She *needed* a cup of tea. Lila appeared two minutes later, slouching in like a sulky teenager. 'What is it, then?'

'I'm — sorry about in there. Sam was digging for information the other day, and being Sam, she decided to drop me in it. She said she'd seen you with someone in the Fiddler.'

Lila snorted. 'She can make what she wants out of it.'

'Is it serious?' Pippa asked.

Lila looked at her feet. 'Dunno. I'd like it to be.'

'Do I get to meet him?'

Lila smiled, a shy smile that Pippa had never seen before. 'Yeah. Not yet, though. I don't think I'm ready for it.'

'It doesn't have to be a big thing —'

'I know. It's just — he's not my usual type. It's taken me a bit by surprise. There I was, heading for mad old lady status, and bam!' Lila's fist hit her palm. But she was grinning.

'Where did you meet?'

'This is going to sound really rubbish…' Lila's feet received another close inspection. 'It was at the bank.'

'Oh, in the queue?'

Lila smirked. 'Behind the counter.'

'Ohhh.' Well, banking was a nice steady job. If he worked on the counter, he definitely wasn't the embezzling fat-cat kind of banker. 'Does he have a name?'

'He does… Stop cross-examining me, Pip. You'll get the dirt, but in my own time. You're the first person I've told.'

'Thanks.' The urn hissed. 'Want a brew?'

'God, yes.'

They sipped their drinks in silence for a few moments, leaning against the worktop side by side. 'How long are you going to keep it quiet?' asked Pippa.

Lila twisted her mouth. 'As long as I can. But with big-gob Sam, I've probably got a week.' She put her cup down and glanced at her phone. 'I'll have to scoot for work in a minute.' She looked at Pippa speculatively. 'I'll ask Jeff if he's all right with meeting you for coffee or something one evening. Out of the village.' She caught Pippa's expression. 'I'm not ashamed of him!'

'No, of course not,' Pippa soothed. 'It's just . . . you seem very protective. I promise I won't interrogate him, if that helps.'

'I'll think it over.' Lila drained her cup. 'I'm not used to caring what other people think,' she mused. 'I've obviously lived here too long.' She checked her watch, then opened the hatch, shouted 'Bella, time to go!', and slammed it. 'See you next week.'

The next thing Pippa heard was the wail of an outraged Ruby. The bang must have startled her. She hurried out and gathered the flailing baby into her arms. 'Sshhh, Ruby, ssshhhh…' She rocked her from side to side as the main door fell closed behind Lila and Bella.

'Honestly,' someone murmured.

Once Ruby had stopped flailing, she snuggled into Pippa and began rooting for milk. 'Come on, then.' Pippa fetched a muslin from her changing bag, found a chair away from the action and sat down. As Ruby fed, she let her thoughts drift. It wasn't exactly the playgroup session she had hoped for; but at least she would get to meet Lila's new man, and they'd managed to resolve matters without a stand-up row. Plus she'd learnt an important lesson. *Don't trust Sam as far as you can throw her, however nice she's being.* Where was Sam? Ah, on the floor playing with Livvy, who looked trapped. *Get a grip, woman.* Then she rebuked herself. It wasn't Sam's fault she was clingy. The nastiness, however, she could work on. And with that rather smug thought, she let her gaze settle on Ruby's gently-bobbing head.

CHAPTER 8

Pippa was in two minds as she drove along the winding road to Lower Gadding. Was the choir really her thing? But Simon had urged her to give it a fair chance. 'One session isn't enough to make your mind up, Pip,' he had said, scanning the fridge for something to eat. 'Isn't there some research about how many times kids have to try new foods before they like them?'

'That's different,' Pippa said, somewhat tersely. 'I'm not a kid.'

Simon gave her a long look, then took a microwave meal out of the fridge and closed the door. 'I didn't say you were. But if you want things to change, you have to be prepared to step out of your comfort zone.'

'I didn't ask for a management lecture,' Pippa retorted, then held her hands up. 'Sorry, but . . . it's not you going into that room, not even sure if you can do it.'

Simon snorted. 'I spend half my working life doing pretty much that.' He slid the cardboard sleeve from the ready meal and peered at it.

'Is that true?'

'Yeah.' He paused, thinking. 'All that merger stuff last

year? I was terrified someone would point at me and shout "You don't know what you're doing, do you?"' He smiled, a little sadly. 'And if they had, it would have been true. But no-one else was doing it.' He opened the drawer for a fork. 'You'd better go, Pip, or you'll be late.'

'Thanks.' Pippa put her arms round Simon's waist and kissed him.

'Any time,' he said, inspecting her. 'You look brighter already. Go on, knock 'em dead.'

If I open my mouth, that'll be a start. At least she knew where to park this time.

Pippa checked her watch as she walked up the path. Seven twenty-five. She had her music folder, and was ready to sing. She breathed out sharply, and opened the door, plastering a 'Here I am!' grin on her face.

No-one noticed her entrance. They were gathered in a group at the far end of the room, talking animatedly, with Jen at the centre. At least they seemed more cohesive this week. No-one was left out, no-one was whispering in corners. Jen's ultimatum must have worked. *There, I was right to come back*, she thought, triumphantly.

Then she caught sight of a couple of faces, and stopped dead.

'What is it? What's happened?' But no-one heard her. She had to go right up to the group before anyone saw her.

'Oh! It's you,' said Edie, frowning as if trying to place her.

'Pippa,' said Pippa.

'Yes. Of course. I'm sorry, dear,' she said, her face softening a little. 'We've had some terrible news.' Someone touched her arm, and she turned to the group to respond.

Pippa stepped back, wondering if she should go, when Gerry caught sight of her and came round the edge of the group. 'You won't have heard, love. It's Claire. Do you remember last week, when we tried that new arrangement and it went wrong?'

'Oh yes,' said Pippa. Had this Claire suddenly lost her voice? Gone tone-deaf?

'Well, if you remember the soloists, Claire was the soprano one. Dark hair, pink cheeks, quite plump...'

'Ohh...' Pippa scanned the group.

'No point looking for her, love,' said Gerry, quietly. 'She died of a heart attack, the night after our last choir practice. Jen's just told us.'

Pippa's mouth dropped open. 'Oh my gosh . . . I'm so sorry.'

'Thank you. She was a lovely girl. Voice of an angel —' Gerry's voice trembled on the last word, and he wiped an eye.

'I take it you weren't expecting...'

'No, no. She was young, in her forties maybe. I don't know if she had heart trouble, it's not the sort of thing we talk about. And Claire wasn't much of a talker anyway. She saved her voice for singing.' Gerry took out a large blue handkerchief and blew his nose. 'I don't know how we're going to get on tonight,' he muttered. 'I don't think I can sing a note.'

Just past Gerry, Pippa saw someone talking to Jen motion in her direction. Jen walked over, gently moving people aside to get through. Her face was pale, and looked paler in contrast with her dark suit. 'Hello, Pippa,' she said, quietly. 'I take it you've heard.'

'Yes, Gerry told me.' Pippa looked round for him, but

Gerry had already moved away, and was talking earnestly to Edie.

'Ah.' Jen seemed hardly to be there. 'It's good that you came back. This isn't normal,' she added. 'We're a quiet community choir. We've never — lost a member before. Anyway, we'd better get on,' she said, with a sudden briskness. 'Excuse me.' She walked to the side of the room and lifted her music stand from its canvas bag. Folded, it resembled a sleeping metal spider.

When the stand was set up, Jen fetched her music and her baton. She did not need to rap the stand, though. Everyone was watching her. 'We have two weeks till the heats,' she said, in her normal voice. 'Claire would have wanted us to get on and practise.' She paused. 'Places, please. Let's sing.'

The only noise for a minute or two was the slap of feet on the floor and the rustle of paper, as everyone got into position. 'Soloists, step forward, please.'

There was a small hubbub among the sopranos. 'What about —?'

Suddenly, Jen looked exhausted. 'Daphne, can you take it?' she muttered.

A formidable woman with elaborate steel-grey hair made her way to the front. 'Yes, Jen. I'll try,' she said, in an unexpectedly sweet voice.

'Thank you.' Jen went to her case and pulled out some sheets of music, pressing them into Daphne's hand. 'I'll need these back at the end — they're the only copy — but I'll get a set to you in the week.' Daphne was already studying the score. 'OK. From the top.'

This time there was no splinter group, no deliberate unfollowing. The choir stayed together. It wasn't perfect —

there were false notes, and the timing wasn't crisp. And yet, while it was considerably better than the week before, something was missing. It wasn't surprising. Daphne sang nicely, but her voice didn't have the arresting quality that Pippa now realised Claire's had possessed. The music drew to a close, and Pippa had been so busy listening that she had completely forgotten to sing herself.

'Well done, everyone,' Jen said. 'Let's have another go. Daphne, how did you find it?'

Daphne shrugged, then smiled. 'I'll get there.'

'I know you will. Pippa?'

Pippa jumped. 'Yes, Jen?'

'Are you getting on OK?'

How did Jen manage to conduct the whole choir and rumble her at the same time? Pippa wished the floor would swallow her up. 'I — think I'm getting there.'

'Good. If you're nervous, hum your part.' Jen smiled encouragingly and tapped the stand. 'After four.'

At least she had permission to keep her mouth shut. The first bit she could definitely do. Pippa leaned as close as she dared to her neighbour to check her pitch. It seemed all right, so she carried on. She felt ridiculous, like an oversized bee. It didn't help that she was wearing a stripy top. But she kept humming. Then a thought popped into her head. *Why am I humming the only song that I know the words to?* She stopped, took a deep breath, and before she could get cold feet, began to sing.

Nobody fainted in horror. Nobody recoiled clutching their ears. In fact, Pippa suspected no-one could hear her over the wall of sound.

She managed to keep up until the soloists started the transition, and then resumed humming. Maybe, if she felt brave, she'd sing the chorus.

It's coming... This, Pippa thought, might be how surfers feel when they're waiting for the big wave to come, when they know they have to seize the moment, stop paddling, and try to catch the wave.

Yes! I'm singing! For those few lines she was part of a huge movement of music, which (whatever your personal opinion of 'Uptown Funk' as a song) was in absolute unison. Pippa sang on, as loud as she could. She actually heard her own voice above that of the choir. And from the lack of elbows in her ribs, she was in time and tune.

She didn't want it to end, but end it must. When they had drawn to a close, and everyone stood silent for a moment, Pippa looked at Jen's sombre face and felt guilty that she had enjoyed it so much.

'That was good,' Jen said. 'Let's take a break. I don't think any of us are up to a full-length rehearsal tonight. Ten minutes for a brew and a comfort break, and then we'll try it one more time before finishing.'

Everyone was still very subdued. Voices were hushed as people queued for their drinks. Someone touched Pippa's arm from behind. 'You seem to be getting into it.'

Pippa turned. The speaker was a slight, mousy-haired woman in jeans and a fluffy jumper. 'Erm, thanks.'

'No problem. It's nice to see someone enjoying themselves singing. I can't say I have tonight.'

'Did you know Claire well?'

The woman nodded vigorously. 'We volunteered at the same charity shop. She told me about the choir. I wouldn't be here if it wasn't for her. And now she's gone. I can't believe it.'

'She wasn't — ill, then?'

'Nooooooo.' The woman shook her head. 'She got a bit breathless occasionally, but she said it was a stress thing. She just used a little spray thingy, and she was fine.'

'Aah.' The queue shuffled forward. 'Did Claire have a stressful job, then?'

'Don't think so. She didn't need to work, but she said she didn't want to fossilise at home.' The woman sniffed. 'This isn't the same without her.' She turned away and rummaged in her bag, then fumbled with a packet of tissues.

Pippa's brain was whirring. A sudden, unexpected death of a woman in her forties, just after a choir practice where she had been chosen as a soloist... It was no kind of motive, but... She longed to probe further, but that was impossible. What on earth would people think if she did?

Pippa did not sing again that evening. She arranged her mouth in the hum position, then kept her eyes on Jen, whose conducting was as brisk and energetic as ever, whatever she felt inside.

'Great. That's a wrap.' Jen's arm fell to her side. 'Let's leave it till next week. I hope we'll all be feeling more like it. But you were great.' She stepped back. 'One more thing. When Pete rang, he asked me to let you know that Claire's funeral service is next Wednesday, eleven o'clock, down the road at St Columba's. I'll be there to give Claire a good send-off, and I hope some of you can come too.'

Pippa fetched her bag and slipped her music into its folder. Several people were lingering, talking it over, sharing their grief. Claire had obviously been a well-regarded member of the choir, someone who many counted as a friend, however reserved she was.

Perhaps it was one of those things. A tragedy of

someone dying young, unexpectedly.

Pippa walked to the door and turned to wish a general good-night, but everyone remaining seemed so absorbed that she did not want to disturb them. She could be friendly next week.

The night air was freezing. Next week she would remember her scarf and gloves. The moon was behind a cloud, and the car park was unlit. What if it was icy? She inched along, testing the tarmac with her trainers.

She was almost at the pavement when she heard a low laugh from the wooden bus shelter. She stopped dead and tried to tune her ears to the buzz of conversation within. Too low. She moved forward, until her ear touched the wood.

'No one could have seen that coming… I'd have put money on Jen. Running the choir for no time, and she throws her weight around like she's Gareth Malone or something.'

A snort. 'Yeah. She'd be no loss.'

'That's how it is, though. It's never the people you'd be happy to see gone.'

'True…' The flick of a cigarette lighter. Pippa longed to find a gap to peep through, but she'd already been standing there long enough. It was pitch black, hopefully too dark for anyone to see her, but you never knew.

Pippa crept away, putting plenty of distance between herself and the shelter before emerging onto the road. The cold of the February night air was completely forgotten. She was burning with speculation, conjecture, and the prospect of a potential murder to solve.

CHAPTER 9

'You're joking.' Simon stared at Pippa, and there was something about his expression that she found uncomfortable.

'I wish I was.' Pippa sat heavily on the sofa and kicked off her shoes. 'It's really fishy. People don't die out of the blue. I was talking to one of her friends in the tea queue and she said Claire was healthy. Just breathless sometimes. And she had a spray. I need to Google that —' She pulled her phone from her bag.

'*No.*'

It was Pippa's turn to stare. 'What do you mean, no? She could have been murdered!'

Simon crossed the room to sit opposite her. He pushed his hair back, and Pippa saw the full extent of his frown. 'I mean — don't do this! Some poor woman you don't even know has just died. You can't go cross-examining her friends because you're bored!'

'It isn't that!' Pippa cried. 'It seems *wrong*. Plus I heard something which confirmed it. People were talking at the bus stop, and one of them said that it was never the people who asked for it. Maybe someone made a mistake, and poisoned the wrong person —'

'Whoa!' Simon held his hands up. 'Someone actually said that to you?'

'Not to me, exactly...' Pippa squirmed under the directness of Simon's look, a butterfly wriggling on a pin. 'I was behind the bus shelter.'

'So you were eavesdropping.'

'I suppose so.'

'Spying.'

'That's not fair!'

'I'm being realistic, Pippa.' Simon leaned forward, hands on knees. 'If someone notices you sneaking around, listening in on private conversations, and pumping people for information, how does that look? Word gets out in a small place like this. You'll probably find yourself with no friends. And you know what? I wouldn't blame them.' He stood up. 'The kids are fine, in case you were wondering,' he threw over his shoulder as he left the room.

Pippa breathed deeply. She wasn't sure how she felt at all. Angry, yes. Wounded, definitely. But she still intended to find out more. If the result convinced her this wasn't a murder, great. It would put her mind at rest and she could get on with her life.

She glanced at the phone on the coffee table. The TV was on, but... She switched the phone into silent mode, keeping an eye on the door.

She typed *breathless spray* into the internet browser.

A stream of perfume adverts. *Try again.*

She added *exercise stress* to her search. *Aha!*

Her eye scanned the results. *GTN spray . . . coronary stent procedure . . . heart attack . . . angina...*

Angina!

A creak from the other room. Pippa just had time to lock the phone and put it down before Simon came in.

'Maybe I was a bit harsh,' he said. 'I'm sorry, Pip.'

'It's OK,' she said. 'I was a bit full-on.'

'Mmm. Death isn't entertainment, you know.'

Pippa looked pointedly at the TV, where Emilia Fox was gazing soulfully at a dead body on the slab.

'You know what I mean,' said Simon testily. 'Don't make me take that apology back.' He picked up the remote and switched to a cookery show.

'Sorry,' said Pippa, as contritely as she could manage.

'Anyway…' Simon sat beside her. 'How was the rest of choir?'

'Good. I sang a bit this week.'

'Do you think you'll still go?'

'Um, yes. Why wouldn't I?'

Simon reached for her hand. 'I don't think you'd be able to resist a bit of questioning, and if you don't go, you won't be tempted.'

'So I can't have a hobby?' Pippa snatched her hand away.

'I didn't say that!' Simon cried. 'I'm trying to protect you!'

'Maybe I don't need protecting,' Pippa growled, getting to her feet. 'Stop shouting, you'll wake the kids up.'

'Fine. Whatever,' Simon said as she flounced upstairs.

Pippa stopped dead and stomped back down. 'Not whatever! If I suspect someone's been murdered, isn't that important? And if they got the wrong person, they might have another go!'

'Take it to the police, then,' Simon said, and she winced at the sharpness in his voice. 'They're qualified to do this.

You're not.'

Pippa went upstairs without another word. As she got ready for bed she turned Simon's response over in her mind. He ought to know that telling her not to do something was exactly the way to make her do it. She toyed with the pleasant notion that this gave her an automatic get-out clause, since Simon's subconscious clearly wanted her to investigate. Halfway through cleaning her teeth, though, she admitted to herself that his reaction was probably what she could expect from everybody else. If not worse.

She spat out the toothpaste, looked at herself in the bathroom mirror, and sighed.

There was nothing for it.

For now, at least, she would have to operate undercover.

***

Pippa could scarcely wait for playgroup to finish the next day. She had hoped to do research on her phone while Freddie played and Ruby got in some quality rolling, but Ruby was fretting. The only thing that would soothe her was standing up and rocking her continuously, until Pippa felt seasick.

'Do you want me to take her for a bit?' Lila looked up from her phone. To be fair, she had chatted to Pippa between texts.

'Oh, would you?' Pippa gently disengaged Ruby's fists from her top.

Lila put her phone on the chair and stood up. 'Come to Auntie Lila then, Ruby-woo. Mind what you're doing with those fists.'

Ruby screwed up her face, which went scarlet, and then

let out a massive fart. 'Better out than in,' said Lila, making a face. 'Thanks for that, Ruby.'

'Sorry,' said Pippa, glad she'd escaped that one. 'I think it runs in the family. Freddie was a nightmare.'

'Mm.' Ruby wailed and Lila inspected the cavern of her mouth. 'I think… Are your hands clean?'

'Yes, Mum.' Pippa peered in. 'What is it?'

'I think Ruby's getting a tooth. Look at her bottom gum.'

The centre of Ruby's lower gum was bright red. Pippa ran her finger along it, feeling the sharp little edge. 'She is! Oh heck, back to teething rings in the fridge and no sleep.' Ruby wailed again and waved her fists. 'I'll have her before she gives you a black eye.'

'Thanks. Not a good look for work.' Lila smoothed her blouse.

'How are things with Jeff?' Pippa asked, under her breath.

'Fine, fine. I mentioned you.'

Pippa paused mid-rock. 'And?'

'Yeah, he's fine with meeting up. Is a Monday or a Wednesday evening OK?'

'Can't do Wednesdays. Monday — I'll have to check with Simon, but yes, probably.' Ruby had stopped kicking her legs, and her body had relaxed a little. 'That's pretty specific.'

'I know. My sister goes out on Friday nights, so she won't babysit. On Tuesdays and Thursdays Jeff does some sort of embarrassing hobby. I keep trying to guess what it is, but he wants to wait until we know each other better before he tells me.'

'Fox hunting? Bear-baiting? Train spotting?'

'I hadn't thought of bear-baiting,' Lila mused. 'It isn't either of the other two. Anyway, he says the embarrassing hobby is quite full-on at the moment.'

'OK, Monday it is.'

'Could you do next Monday?' Lila put her hand on Pippa's arm. 'I do want you to meet him. I'd be really interested to know what you think.'

'Should be fine.' Simon would probably be happy that Lila was chaperoning her.

The serving hatch doors creaked open. 'Snack time!' Caitlin called.

'Oh no!' Lila grabbed her bag. 'Late again. Bella!' Bella slouched over, looking more like a tiny teenager than ever in her Ramones T-shirt. 'Text me,' she mouthed. 'Bye, Ruby!'

Pippa spent the rest of the session failing to sit down. Every time she began lowering herself onto a chair, Ruby's eyes opened and she started to grizzle. On the one occasion both Pippa's buttocks touched a seat, Ruby responded by filling her nappy. It was a relief to strap her into her pushchair and round up Freddie at the end of the morning.

'Tearoom?' prompted Freddie.

'Maybe.' Pippa manoeuvred Ruby out of the door. 'They may not have the beans you like either, you know.'

'I might try something else,' said Freddie.

'What?' Pippa stared at her son. 'In all the times we've gone to the tearoom you have never, ever, eaten a meal without beans.'

'Mrs M says vari-ty is important.'

'Good for Mrs M. Anyway, we're going somewhere else first.'

'Where? Where?' Freddie demanded, looking up into

her face.

'The library.'

'Ooh, is it story time?'

'I could read you a story.'

'Mrs M says the town library has story times,' Freddie declared. 'Someone reads a story, and there's music, and activities.'

'Ahh, that word again. We'll have to make do.' Pippa didn't exactly wish harm on Mrs M, but if she could just stop giving Freddie ideas, that would be wonderful.

By the time they got to the library Ruby was lolling sideways in her pushchair, fast asleep. Pippa put a finger to her lips. 'Can you hold the door, Freddie?' He obliged, grinning, and she wheeled Ruby into the tiny foyer and through to the library.

As she had hoped, the library was empty except for Norm, who had his nose buried in a thriller.

Freddie pulled her sleeve. 'Can I choose books, Mummy?'

'Of course, but be quiet.' Pippa parked Ruby and walked to the far end of the library; a matter of eight small steps.

Norm looked up. 'Hello, stranger!'

Pippa pointed to the sleeping Ruby.

'Ohhh. Sorry,' he stage-whispered. 'Have you brought *Styles* back?'

'I haven't had time to finish it,' Pippa admitted, sitting on the plastic chair in front of the desk.

Norm raised his eyebrows.

'I haven't! I hardly get time to read the cereal packet with a three-month old in the house. Not to speak of Freddie.' She glanced at the children's section, where

Freddie was sitting nicely on a beanbag, absorbed in a book. *Thanks, kiddo.* She leaned forward and lowered her voice. 'And there's something else.'

Norm picked up a bookmark from the desk and closed his book. 'What sort of something else?' he said. His voice was quiet, but Pippa knew that he had taken the bait. She summarised what she had learnt the night before, then sat back and looked at him expectantly.

'Mm,' said Norm.

'What do you mean, mm?' Pippa put her elbows on the desk. 'Doesn't it sound weird to you?'

'Unusual, yes. But these things happen, unfortunately.' Norm steepled his fingers and looked over them at her. 'As an ex-copper myself, I don't think this would set my alarm bells ringing. For one thing, where's the motive?'

'But if they killed the wrong person, that wouldn't matter.'

'And how exactly did someone kill her?' Norm said patiently. 'I'm not being awkward, Pippa, but you need facts. Or at least possibilities.'

'I haven't managed to research that bit yet,' said Pippa. 'I am quite busy, you know. In fact, I could use some help with that.' She raised her eyebrows at Norm, but he shook his head.

'One thing I learnt as a policeman, and you won't like this, was to keep my nose out unless I was sure a matter warranted sticking it in.' He held up a hand as Pippa opened her mouth. 'Hear me out. In order to establish that this woman didn't die of natural causes, someone would have to do a post-mortem. That won't happen unless her doctor considers the death unexpected enough to order one. That won't be the case, as the lady had been diagnosed with heart trouble. You also said that the choir meeting was fraught. Angina attacks can be caused by stress. It isn't difficult to put two and two together, is it?'

'No,' muttered Pippa.

'So in order to get a post-mortem ordered, you would have to give the police — not me, the real police — actual cause to suspect that there was foul play. What you've got just won't cut it.'

'Read me a story, Mummy,' Freddie piped from the beanbag.

Pippa swallowed. 'Of course.' She got up, seething inwardly. How dare Norm dismiss her! But she could feel herself blushing. He made it sound so stupid, as if she was trying to pluck murders out of thin air.

She sat down with Freddie and read him *The Very Hungry Caterpillar*. Norm had wandered to the bookcases and was examining a shelf, muttering to himself.

'I'm hungry, Mummy,' said Freddie, as she closed the book. 'Can we go for lunch now?'

'Do you want to choose a couple of books to take home, Freddie?'

'Noooo,' Freddie moaned. 'I'm too huuuuungry…'

'OK.' Pippa got up, with difficulty, and walked over to Ruby. Her cheeks were taking on that flushed, shiny look she remembered from Freddie's teething days.

'Before you go —' Norm hurried over with a small stack of books. 'These'll take your mind off things. Let me know how you get on with them.'

Pippa examined the books. *Appointment with Death, Crooked House, Curtain*. 'I know I've read this one,' she said, holding up *Curtain*. 'I might have read the others, too.'

'They'll bear rereading,' said Norm, strolling to his desk. 'Enjoy your lunch.'

Freddie had cheese on toast at the tearoom, and their cheese was, apparently, not as cheesy as preschool's. Pippa ordered a ham and brie croissant and a cappuccino, which she consumed as a soggy conglomerate after Ruby upended her cup with a well-aimed thrash. It seemed even minor indulgence was off-limits, unless this was some sort of karma for sticking her nose in. Either way, she felt thoroughly chastised.

CHAPTER 10

'Have you been spring cleaning?' Sheila asked pleasantly, as she stepped over the threshold. 'Everything looks very fresh.'

'Can you keep your voice down, please?' Pippa groaned. 'Ruby's just fallen asleep and I'm shattered.'

'Oh, I'm sorry,' said Sheila, in slightly less bell-like tones. 'Where's Freddie?'

'He's at preschool. Probably eating caviar or haggis. I need to fetch him at twelve thirty.'

'Oh?' Sheila's face softened. 'Oh dear. Come and sit down,' she said graciously, leading the way into Pippa's sitting room. 'You do look tired.'

'Ruby's teething,' said Pippa, flatly. 'She woke up at half past four this morning and wouldn't sleep. I ended up bringing the Moses basket in here and lying on the floor with her so Simon could get some rest.'

'I'll put the kettle on,' said Sheila. Pippa stared in disbelief at her pink woollen back as she left the room.

She was stiff, and chilly. It probably didn't help that she had spent much of the weekend cleaning. Simon had joked that it was worse than nesting, but Pippa found it calming to wipe the door frames and tackle the cobwebs and even clean the oven. It felt as if she was scrubbing away the cross looks, the reasoning of why she was wrong to suspect anything, the insinuations that she wasn't a nice person.

OK, maybe she wasn't a nice person all the time. But at least with cleaning you could see results. Unlike running, which made you hot and tired after only a few minutes. Plus if she was at home she couldn't be accused of sticking her nose into anything. Simon had gone from joking to looking concerned as the weekend wore on and Pippa moved from room to room with her cleaning cloths and bucket, but he had said nothing.

The library books remained unopened on Pippa's bedside table. She was too tired to think, much less read. Hopefully it would pass, but she had had her fill of mysteries for now, thank you very much.

Sheila advanced into the room balancing two china cups. 'Here you are.' She sat down herself, and sighed. 'So Freddie's at preschool, then.'

'Yes, he loves it. Wants to go on Fridays, too.' Pippa sipped her scalding tea.

'The excitement will wear off,' said Sheila, putting her cup down. 'I remember when Simon went to school. He was so excited. He woke me up at six o'clock, all ready in his little uniform, asking if it was time yet. He loved it. And when I went to collect him on Friday afternoon he was standing in the playground sobbing his heart out, because his teacher had said she'd see him on Monday. He thought it was just for a week, like a holiday.' She smiled fondly, and then her eye fell on Pippa's music folder. 'What's this?' she said, lifting the flap.

'I've joined the choir,' said Pippa. 'Sweet Harmony.'

She had got the folder out intending to hum through her parts while Ruby slept, but it would have to wait.

'Oh, have you?' Sheila's mouth turned down a little. 'They're very modern, aren't they? Janet from bridge club dragged me to one of their concerts...' The corners of her mouth twisted lower, as if the memory was lemon-sour. 'I'm sure they're talented, but give me a proper church choir any day of the week. They started quite well, and then they did this, what is it, hippy-hoppy thing.' Suddenly she brightened. 'But I don't suppose you know...'

'Know what?' said Pippa, cautiously. She'd had enough insinuating conversations lately to last a lifetime.

'About Janet's daughter, poor dear Claire.'

'I heard last night at choir practice,' Pippa said, trying to impart an air of closure to the phrase.

But Sheila was off. 'Such a tragedy . . . Janet's in shock. She didn't come to bridge, which is entirely understandable, but Joan told us. Claire was only forty-six, you know. No age. I don't know how her husband's going to manage, with a young family to bring up. Janet told me he works all hours.'

'Did you know Claire well, then?'

Sheila shook her head regretfully. 'She'd pop in and out of Janet's house with the children, but no, I didn't know her to talk to. She seemed nice, but very busy.' Sheila looked disapproving again. 'Always dashing somewhere or other. Perhaps that's what caused it. I don't know, these have-it-all women.' She eyed the music folder. 'Will you go to the funeral, dear?'

'Oh, um, I don't know.' Pippa frowned. 'I hadn't even really met her.'

'But the choir are going, aren't they? Freddie will be at

preschool, and I could help you keep Ruby quiet.' Sheila put a hand on Pippa's knee. 'It would be a nice gesture,' she said, firmly. 'There's nothing worse than a funeral with hardly anyone there. It makes you feel so sorry for the departed. And the family, of course.'

'It's not as if I have anything else to do,' said Pippa, slowly. Something was stirring inside her, the something she had tried to scrub out of herself all weekend.

Curiosity.

'That's settled, then,' Sheila said comfortably. 'I'll meet you here on Wednesday at half ten. You can drive us, then leave after the service to pick Freddie up, and I'll go to the reception. I'm sure someone will give me a lift.' She looked almost gleeful at the prospect. 'Ooh, you'll be picking Freddie up soon. I'll let you get on.' Sheila got up and trotted into the hall. 'Oh, this is new! How lovely!' She pointed at the photograph of Freddie in the river, which Simon had got printed out and put in a black box frame. 'I didn't know you'd had a portrait session.'

'We haven't,' said Pippa. 'A — friend took it.'

'Well, your friend can take a picture of me any time,' Sheila said, inclining her head graciously. 'I'll see you on Wednesday.' Her eyes travelled over Pippa's faded jeans and baggy cardigan. 'I'm sure you'll be able to find something appropriate to wear. Give Ruby a kiss from Granny, won't you.'

Pippa closed the door quietly behind her, then crossed to the photograph. She still hadn't emailed Serendipity to say thank you. On impulse she pulled out her phone, searched for the email, and pressed *Reply*.

What to write?

Hi Serendipity. The phone wanted to autocorrect to

Serenade, but she overrode it.

Thanks for sending the photo. It's beautiful. I've put it up in the hall. Freddie's grandma has just been admiring it.

Thanks again, Pippa.

There. She checked for spelling mistakes and then pressed *Send* before she could start obsessing over it.

Should I have invited her for coffee?

Oh well, the email was sent. She checked her watch. Five past twelve.

Pippa went up to the bedroom and inspected the contents of her wardrobe. There was a black skirt suit, but she hadn't worn it since her work days. At least with a long top no-one would be able to see the waist straining. She found a plain white shirt to go over it. If she gave Ruby a good feed beforehand, she might sleep through the service. In any case, she could slip out if she sat near the back. She had a sneaking suspicion, though, that Sheila would want to be near the front.

Why is Sheila so keen for me to go? Pippa mused on the question for a while. Some of her answers were rather uncharitable; not that she planned on sharing them.

Pippa riffled through the hangers. Never mind Wednesday, what was she going to wear tonight to meet Lila and the mysterious Jeff? They had arranged to meet in the Rambler's Rest, a country pub outside Upper Gadding. Pippa had never visited before, but the name sounded casual. Jeans and a smart top would probably be fine. She liked the idea of wearing clothes to go out in, as opposed to whatever was currently clean and more or less fitted.

She stiffened at a whimper from Ruby. *Here we go again.*

If she hurried, they could walk to fetch Freddie. But Ruby's whimper became a bellow. Her nappy had filled, and also sprung a leak. Pippa carried the thrashing baby to the changing mat, keeping her at arm's length, and unwrapped the horror. A thorough clean and a change of clothes was required.

Car it is, then. Ruby's cry had taken on an additional 'feed me' note. 'I'm sorry, but you'll have to wait a few minutes,' Pippa told the furious little scarlet face, and carried her to her car seat.

Twenty-five past twelve. Plenty of time.

She turned out of the driveway and saw the bin lorry crawling along twenty feet ahead. Aargh! After drumming her fingers on the steering wheel for what seemed like forever, Pippa executed a slightly erratic three-point turn which made Ruby scream. The long way round was only another minute or two.

Pippa drove to the primary school with no further incidents, but the few spaces by the little wooden hut were already occupied. Pippa considered blocking someone in, and rejected the idea. She eventually found a safe place fifty metres away, released Ruby, and galloped to the preschool, bowed by the weight of the car seat.

Mrs Marks was already at the door. 'Here you are!' she said, with a note of reproach in her voice.

Freddie was sniffling beside her. 'You forgot me!'

'I got stuck behind the dustmen,' Pippa said. 'I'm one minute late.'

'We'll overlook it this time,' said Mrs Marks. 'Normally a fine is payable, but I'm sure you won't do it again.'

'Not if I'll get fined,' Pippa retorted, then reflected that she probably didn't sound at her most maternal. 'Come on Freddie, let's go home. Ruby's hungry.'

'Do we have to?' Freddie stuck his bottom lip out.

'I thought you were desperate to be picked up.' Pippa raised a hand to Mrs Marks and walked down the path. Perhaps she could have a little snooze if both children had a nap at the same time. Otherwise she'd be falling asleep over her glass of Diet Coke tonight.

CHAPTER 11

'Are you sure you'll be able to find it?' Simon asked, standing on the doorstep.

'Satnav,' said Pippa, holding up her phone.

'Be careful, it's in the sticks. Park close to the door.' Simon surveyed her critically. 'You look very nice,' he said at last.

'Thank you.' Pippa was pleased that he'd noticed.

'You'll probably stick out like a sore thumb. Last time I went in it was full of old men and dogs.'

'I think you're meant to wish me a lovely evening,' Pippa said, getting into the car.

'Say hi to Lila,' he responded, closing the door.

Pippa drove carefully, conscious that she was tired. A great deal of under-eye concealer had gone into her preparations. Perhaps a night out would liven her up.

A night out! She had been surprised at how readily Simon had agreed. 'Of course you can go,' he'd said, into the saucepan he was stirring.

'Thank you.' Pippa slid her arms around him. 'Sorry to ask twice in a week.'

'I'm sure you'll return the favour some time.' Simon

turned round and kissed her, briefly, before returning to his pan.

'In 4 miles, take the next left.' Pippa blinked. She was out of the 30-miles-an-hour zone, but she didn't want to race down the country roads. She increased her speed to 50. Hopefully Lila and Jeff, assuming they were travelling together, would be there first. Walking into an unfamiliar pub in the back of beyond wasn't really her thing.

'In 2 miles, take the next left.' It was dark, and the road was unlit. Pippa became aware of buzzing behind her, and headlights on full beam. *They'll dip them in a minute, when they see me.*

The lights advanced rapidly, and the buzz grew into a roar. Pippa's eyes watered, and she adjusted her mirror to reduce the dazzle. The whole interior of the car was cold, bright light.

The car screamed past and Pippa gripped the wheel, hard. She wanted to wipe her eyes but feared irreparable damage. Ahead, the car zoomed into the night. It was large, dark and expensive-sounding, and she hoped she wouldn't encounter it ever again.

'In 1 mile, take the next left.' Now the danger was over, she giggled at the robot voice. What would Jeff be like? Well, she'd find out soon. Half a mile . . . 100 yards . . . turn left…

'You have reached your destination.'

Pippa manoeuvred the Mini into the narrow entrance to the car park. The pub itself was well-lit, with white lights tucked under the thatched roof. *The Rambler's Rest* was written on the cream-washed wall in flowing script, with *Country Pub and Kitchen* added beneath in square capitals.

Hmm. When had Simon last visited? And the car park

was quite full.

Pippa parked and inspected herself in the rear-view mirror. Still presentable, thank heavens. She got out of the Mini, congratulating herself on choosing black leather ankle boots over trusty but battered trainers, and slammed the door. As she walked through the car park and climbed the stone steps to the back door of the pub, she couldn't help noticing that the cars she passed were mainly of the large and expensive variety. Two Bentleys, a couple of BMW sports cars, a sleek Mercedes, and a pugnacious-looking Audi.

The pub itself turned out to be the dim varnished-floorboard and leather-sofa kind. There was no blaring music, just the hum of conversation, with an occasional braying laugh. It was arranged in room-style spaces, and Pippa drifted from room to room, looking for Lila's curly hair.

'Pip!'

No wonder her gaze had slid right over her. Lila had straightened her hair, which flowed shinily past her shoulders. 'Wow, I hardly recognised you!' said Pippa.

'This is Jeff,' Lila said, waving a hand at the man seated next to her. As far as Pippa could tell in the half-light, Jeff was slim, in his early-to-mid thirties, with a dark fringe and black-framed glasses. He was wearing a suit and tie. 'Jeff, this is my friend Pippa.'

'Pleased to meet you, Pippa.' Jeff extended a hand. His voice wavered a little, and his palm was slightly clammy.

'Pleased to meet you too, Jeff. Have you come from work?'

'No,' he said, sounding puzzled.

'Oh. Um, I'll get a drink.'

'No no, I'll go.' He unfolded himself from the sofa. 'What would you like?'

'Just a Diet Coke, please, I'm driving.'

'Coming up.' He smiled, which made him look eighteen. It was a good thing she hadn't ordered wine; the bar staff might have asked him for ID.

'Have you been here a while?' Pippa asked Lila, who had poured herself into a slinky knee-length dress. She felt hopelessly underdressed by comparison.

'Half an hour,' said Lila. She leaned forward. 'What do you think?'

'We've said hello!' Pippa laughed. 'It's a bit early to judge.'

Jeff returned with Pippa's Diet Coke and a slate of nibbles; olives, chorizo, artichokes and cubes of feta cheese. 'This is nice,' said Pippa. 'Not quite the packet of peanuts Simon used to treat me to.'

'I can get you some peanuts,' Jeff said anxiously.

'No! This is lovely.' Pippa popped an olive into her mouth, and bit down on a stone. 'Excuse me,' she muttered, looking for somewhere to put the stone and settling on a spare beermat. 'Can't take me anywhere.'

Lila snorted. 'You could spit them into the fireplace.' Jeff's horrified face made her giggle even more.

The conversation stumbled through films they'd seen lately (not many except for Jeff, who liked blockbusters), what they'd done that weekend (not much, in all cases), and their favourite kinds of food (Jeff favoured a roast dinner, but didn't look as if he'd eaten many of those recently). Pippa eyed Jeff's thin, pale hands, which lay one over the other. No sign of a wedding ring, though of course lots of men didn't wear them. However, she had a feeling that if Jeff were married it would be to the kind of woman who would expect him to wear one. So that was all right.

But she couldn't work out what Lila saw in him. He was pleasant, polite, attentive. He wasn't particularly unattractive, although his nervousness did him no favours. He wasn't creepy.

But is that enough?

Jeff excused himself. Lila watched him walk sedately in the direction of the toilets, then turned to Pippa. 'He's very nervous. He's not normally like this.' Her tone held a faint note of accusation.

'How long have you been seeing each other?'

Lila twisted a glossy strand of hair. 'Six weeks. Ish.'

And already he was staying over, if the car outside Lila's house was anything to go on. 'He seems fine,' Pippa said, keeping her voice light. 'You have my blessing.'

Maybe Lila would get bored with him. Unless Jeff was a charisma dynamo when they were alone. Somehow she doubted it. 'Why him?' she asked.

Lila leaned forward. 'He's nice, and decent, and he makes me feel safe,' she said. 'That's probably dull as dishwater, but after Doug,' — she stuck her tongue out — 'that's worth a lot. Bella likes him, too.'

'He's met Bella?' *Wow, this has gone further than I realised.*

'I've introduced him. Only as a friend. She's far too young to understand.'

'What are his views on kids?' Pippa hesitated. 'I assume he doesn't have any.'

'God, no!' Lila hooted. 'He's fine. I think. He's good with Bella. He talks to her very seriously, and she isn't a little madam like she can be —' She broke off as Jeff returned.

'We should probably head back soon, Lila,' he said. 'I have an early start tomorrow.'

Lila grinned. 'Is the bank opening early?'

Jeff looked confused. 'No, it's opening at nine thirty as usual. But I usually go to the gym before work on a Tuesday.'

'I didn't have you down as a gym bunny, Jeff,' Pippa grinned.

Jeff smiled shyly. 'I like to keep in shape.'

'You could go after work. Oh no, you've got your . . . thing,' said Lila.

'Yes.' He stood waiting until Lila took the hint, drained her glass of wine, and stood up. 'Thanks for coming, Pippa,' he said, rather formally. 'It was nice to meet you.' He paused, then held out his hand.

Pippa shook it, biting back her giggles. 'You too, Jeff.' She thought about saying that they must do it again some time, but to be honest, she could wait.

Jeff took Lila's arm. Pippa followed, and watched them get into a grey Skoda. *Very sensible*. She got into the Mini and turned on the hot air to clear the windscreen. The Skoda's lights came on, dipped, and it moved smoothly past her. She could just see Lila waving from the passenger seat.

By a strange coincidence 'Bohemian Rhapsody' came on the radio as Pippa was pulling out of the car park. She sang along, cruising at a steady 45, tapping the steering wheel lightly to the beat. She felt much happier than she had when she set out. Jeff definitely wasn't married, and he didn't seem like a rat or a druggie. He was a nice, clean-living young man. Not exactly a sex bomb, but OK. She could imagine him being handy with a screwdriver, good at wrangling a pushchair. She was still curious about the mystery hobby, but she suspected it was nothing worse than Dungeons and Dragons, or a bit of light carpentry.

There were no more road hogs on the return journey, and Pippa pulled into the driveway with a sigh of relief.

'You're early,' Simon called from the sitting room. 'It's only half nine.'

'I know. Jeff has to work out in the morning.'

'Does he now.' Simon came into the hall, holding a glass of wine. 'So. What did you think?'

Pippa shrugged. 'He seems all right. Might ease up a bit when he's used to me.'

Simon laughed. 'Did you scare him?'

'I didn't mean to!' Pippa said, indignantly. 'He was a bit rabbit in headlights, though. Oh, and someone tried to mow me down on the road out. Headlights on full, doing about eighty. It reminded me why I don't like driving at night.'

'That's just once in a way, don't let it put you off.' Simon offered the glass of wine.

'Better not. Ruby will want a feed soon, I expect. Afterwards — oh yes.'

Pippa removed her make-up and changed into her pyjamas, then took a book from the top of her reading pile on the bedside table before joining Simon on the sofa.

'What have you got there?' He leaned over to examine the cover. '*Appointment with Death*. Oh, another Agatha. Surely you've read them all.'

'Doesn't matter,' said Pippa. 'I could read them all again, no problem. OK, there are a few I'd skip…'

'So long as the murder stays fictional,' said Simon,

rubbing her knee and turning his gaze to the TV.

Pippa cast a regretful eye at his glass of wine before settling to her book. Maybe Ruby would wake soon, and then she would be able to indulge, too. She read on, becoming absorbed in the story.

'Wow,' Simon's voice made her jump. 'You're devouring that.'

Pippa closed the book on her finger. 'It's very interesting.'

'Good choice, then,' he said, reaching for the wine.

'I didn't choose it,' said Pippa. She stared into the distance for a while. Either it was a complete coincidence, or Norm was the sneakiest librarian in the whole of Gadcestershire.

CHAPTER 12

Sheila ran her eyes appraisingly over Pippa. 'You look nice, dear. Very suitable.' She herself was in a black shift dress, with black stilettos, a clutch bag, and a small black hat. Pippa couldn't decide whether she was dressed for a funeral or a party. 'Are you ready to go?'

Pippa looked down at her black suit, which seemed even more of a make-do. 'I think so. Let me get Ruby into her car seat.' Pippa lifted Ruby and kissed her before putting her in. Unsure of baby funeral dress code, she had put Ruby into her best pale blue frock. It would probably attract some sort of stain, but Pippa was resigned to the inevitable. 'Are you sure they won't mind me bringing her?'

'Of course not,' said Sheila, stepping back to let Pippa out.

Pippa opened the door for Sheila, who descended into the Mini, then strapped Ruby in. As she drove, observing the speed limit at all times, she wondered why Sheila was so keen for her to come. Perhaps she would find out when they got to the church.

St Columba's was not what Pippa had imagined. She

had envisaged a spidery, Gothic church, but St Columba's was a modern red-brick building with a squat tower and abstract stained glass.

'I fear guitars,' Sheila muttered as they picked their way across the car park. 'And clapping.' She sniffed.

Two people were waiting at the porch; a tall, thin, fiftyish man with cropped greying hair, who seemed comfortable in his suit, and a shorter, plump woman of the same age. 'That's Pete,' hissed Sheila. 'I don't know who the woman is. Maybe a sister?'

Pete stepped forward, his hand out and a sad smile coming readily to his face. How many times had he done this today? 'Sheila, hello. Thank you for coming. Janet will be glad to see you.'

Sheila preened a little as she pressed his hand. 'I'll go in and say a few words.' Her feet tapped over the parquet floor, leaving Pippa behind.

Pete's left eyebrow quirked up slightly. 'I don't think we've met?'

'Er, no, sorry. I'm Pippa. I'm part of the choir…'

'Ohhh, of course. Yes, Claire loved to sing.'

'I hope it's all right for me to bring Ruby.' They both looked at the car seat, where Ruby was busy investigating her own fingers.

'Oh yes, of course. There are a few babies with us today.' He sighed. 'Claire would have loved that. She always wanted a large family.'

Pippa nodded. There were so many questions she would love to ask, but now was definitely not the time. Perhaps Sheila would be able to supply further information, after the funeral . . . oh, that sounded awful. 'I'd better go in,' she gabbled, feeling her face grow hot. 'It was lovely to meet you.'

'You too,' said Pete, holding his hand out to her. Pippa took it, and instead of the firm handshake she had expected, received a gentle press. His hand was not what she had expected, either. Weren't surveyors hands-on sorts of people, getting busy with tools? Pete's hand was soft, the nails well-shaped. She noted, also, that his shirt was fastened with intricate gold cufflinks.

The woman, who was engaged with another guest, smiled at Pippa as she went in. Pippa strained her ears and was rewarded with 'I'm Claire's sister, Carolyn.' Her voice was soft. Had Claire been as softly spoken? Pippa didn't know. She'd never heard Claire speak, even. Yet here she was, assuming the poor woman had been murdered.

'Come along, Ruby,' she said as she walked into the church, more to calm her own nerves than anything. She glimpsed the coffin, topped with flowers. The front rows were full — the church had chairs, not pews. Pippa scanned them for Sheila's little black hat, and saw it, eventually, in the second row. Sheila was deep in conversation with a similarly-attired woman sitting in the front row. That must be Janet. All the chairs round Sheila were occupied. *Thanks.*

Perhaps it was a good thing. She could sit further back and observe. And if she got an aisle seat (which Ruby would justify), she would have a good view of most of the rows. Pippa spied one on the right hand side and walked towards it.

'Pssst!' That couldn't be meant for her.

A hand touched her elbow, and Pippa jumped.

'This side,' said Edie. 'We'll make room. Move up, girls.' With a great deal of shuffling and whispering, the row moved along. From what Pippa could see, every woman in the row was from the alto section.

'Where are the sopranos?' she asked.

'Across the aisle,' said Edie, passing her an order of service. 'And the tenors and basses are split too, behind us.'

'Is Jen here?'

'Of course.' Edie pointed to Jen, in an aisle seat a few rows ahead, wearing her usual black trouser suit. 'Keep an eye on her when the hymns start.'

Pippa looked at her watch. Two minutes to eleven. A few stragglers were coming in. Ruby was wide-eyed but mercifully silent. Pippa hoped the hymns wouldn't set her off crying. Then again, if they did Ruby would probably be inaudible above a choir at full strength.

Almost full strength.

Pete hurried past, so quickly that the breeze made Ruby's car seat tremble. Carolyn followed, more sedately. Both took their seats in the front row, and the priest came forward.

'Hymn 164,' he intoned. 'Please rise.'

'Father George,' Edie muttered. 'He's very good. Buried most of my family.'

Pippa got to her feet, unaccountably nervous, and found the hymn in her book. At least it was one she knew, though if it had an alto part she was unaware of it.

Edie put a hand on her trembling arm. 'Just sing the standard version, it'll be fine.' The organ rang out, and Edie puffed up like a white-haired robin.

The choir took the roof off. Pippa needn't have worried; she couldn't hear herself at all. She mouthed the words and looked for Jen, who was beating time very gently. When her right thumb dipped, the booming of the basses diminished. Her left fingers moved upwards, and the altos climbed accordingly. What on earth must her neighbours make of it? But Claire, surely, would have approved, and that was what mattered. Pippa relaxed and let herself enjoy the music. The organ played the closing notes, and a triumphant silence hung in the air.

Pippa let the gospel readings wash over her as she watched the congregation, occasionally glancing at Ruby, who was being good as gold. There were other babies and young children present, probably a result of a midweek funeral, and gurgles and cries came from all parts of the room. They didn't derail the reader, whose voice rolled on like a soothing wave.

Pippa studied the front row. Pete, Janet . . . was that Carolyn next to Janet? She couldn't be sure. There was a line of similar, roundish shoulders. Claire seemed to be one of many. In the middle were two smaller, thinner shapes. The children. Pippa bit her lip. How terrible to lose your mother at such a young age. How would Pete cope, if he worked away so much? Perhaps he would have to change jobs...

Another hymn — luckily Ruby was fast asleep, heaven knows how — and on to prayers and responses, which required Pippa's attention even with an order of service to guide her.

Then the priest called Pete up. He spoke simply, confidently, about Claire; how they had met, her hobbies and interests, her voluntary work, their children. 'We were married for fifteen happy, happy years,' he said, pursing his mouth up as if to hold it steady. 'I wish it had been longer, but — the Lord's will.'

There were a few murmurs in the congregation at that, and Father George surveyed the room with a steely eye until there was quiet.

Pete said a few more conventional words and walked to his seat, eyes downcast. Pippa wasn't sure what she had been expecting — she hadn't attended enough funerals to know, which surely was a blessing. Just before he turned to sit, Pete's heavy-lidded eyes flicked to the right, and he shook his head slightly.

What was that about?

Carolyn stood up next and spoke of Claire's childhood and how close they were as a family, with five sisters and one brother living within ten miles of each other and the family home. Carolyn's address was more halting than Pete's, and there were pink blotches on her neck. Once or twice she excused herself to take a sip of water. It was hardly surprising. Some people hated speaking in front of an audience, and when it was your own sister…

Close, or claustrophobic? Pippa frowned at herself even as she thought it.

Now the service seemed to be building up to a climax. It hadn't gone on for long, but then the death had been unexpected. Perhaps this was the only slot they could get, with no time to plan.

Unless someone *had* planned…

People were rising, and the organ groaned into life. Ruby, who had slumbered so peacefully throughout, opened her eyes in fright and her limbs jerked as if she had been shocked. Pippa lifted her out of the car seat, but Ruby screamed again and again, unplacatable. Pippa strapped her in and carried her away, thankful at least that the cause of Ruby's upset was also drowning her out.

Pippa settled down in the back seat of the Mini with Ruby. Her screams had faded to whimpers as they got further from the crashing organ, but Ruby's arms and legs were still waving, and she looked as if she had had a nightmare. Pippa closed the car door, found a muslin, and unbuttoned her blouse, hoping a quick feed would make her happier. She had ten minutes until she would need to fetch Freddie. Ruby put a little hand on Pippa's breast and cooed. Seconds later, she was latched on.

The coffin nosed its way out of the church, carried by six men. Pete's suit was at the head. Who were the others? Her brother, her father? Perhaps brothers in law… The priest followed, and the congregation were straggling out now. Pippa could see Jen, dabbing at her eyes with a hanky. The long tail started to break, and dribs and drabs of people brought up the rear. One more . . . and one more…

Then nothing. That must be it.

The sucking ceased. Pippa looked down. Ruby batted at her gently, which Pippa took to mean that she had finished. 'You can have the other side later,' she told the baby, buttoning up. She draped the muslin over her shoulder and patted Ruby's back gently to wind her. A little strangled burp came out.

'There's a good girl,' Pippa said absently, continuing to pat.

Ruby seemed to gather herself up, and a huge rasping burp echoed round the car.

'Wow!' Pippa checked the muslin to be certain Ruby hadn't thrown up, but it was innocent.

She caught a slight movement out of the corner of her eye. A slim black-clothed figure was hurrying down the path to the street. Pippa couldn't see her face, but her command of platform heels and the flexibility of her gait suggested she was in her thirties or less. Her hair was dark and gathered in a large bun on top of her head. She took something from her bag — a phone? — and disappeared from view.

Aargh! Pippa bumped her head gently against the seat in front of her. *An interesting woman sneaks off instead of going to the graveside, and I can't follow her!* She felt a tug on her shirt. Ruby was gazing up at her, a dribble of milk running down her chin.

'I bet Miss Marple never had this sort of thing,' she said. 'Let's go and get your brother.' She opened the car door, balancing Ruby on her lap, then got out to arrange the car seat.

She could just see the group gathered round the grave, the priest standing a little apart. Pippa shivered. She was glad to be missing this bit. At least —

She choked the thought off, adjusted the seat, and strapped Ruby in, before getting in herself and starting the engine. She did a three-point turn and drove away.

At least it wasn't a cremation, and if they did need to dig up —

Stop it, Pippa!

She switched the radio on and turned it up. Now was not the time to be thinking like this.

But was there a right time?

Or was she clutching at straws?

CHAPTER 13

It seemed strange to be driving back to Lower Gadding again. At least this time Pippa wasn't trussed up in a suit. She had made it to preschool in the nick of time, with no choice but to block someone in or risk a fine. Pippa unbuckled Ruby and ran up the path as fast as she could in heels, leaning on the bell.

'Ah, here she is,' said Mrs Marks comfortably, reaching up to unbolt the door. 'Come on, Freddie.'

'Can't I stay a bit longer?' said Freddie.

'No dear, it's time to go.'

'Hello Pippa.'

Pippa would have known that voice anywhere. 'Hello, Sam.'

'You're looking smart today. Been somewhere?'

'Yes, I have.' Pippa held her hand out to Freddie, who took it rather unwillingly. 'Has he been good, Mrs Marks?'

'Of course!' she beamed. 'Haven't you, munchkin?'

Munchkin. That's new.

'Well, I can't stand here gossiping,' said Sam. 'Time to go, Livvy.'

Livvy was sitting in the middle of the rug, stacking

blocks into a tower. 'Nooooo…' she wailed, and swiped the tower down.

'Yes!' Sam walked across and picked her up. Livvy put her thumb in her mouth and sucked it venomously as her mother bore her off, calling 'Bye, Mrs Marks!' over her shoulder.

'I thought Livvy couldn't stand to be away from her mum for a full session,' Pippa said, meditatively.

Mrs Marks snorted. 'Other way round, if you ask me. That isn't my professional opinion, you understand,' she added, hastily.

Pippa smiled. 'Of course not.'

Following the morning's excitement, the afternoon fell a little flat. Pippa would have loved to visit Sheila to try and get some juice on the reception, but that would have required more front than Blackpool. So she spent the hours until Simon came home in reducing the washing pile, cooking bolognese sauce for later, and keeping the children sort of entertained, with the invaluable assistance of SuperMouse. The suit was in the wardrobe, the shirt already spinning round in a mixed load, and Simon need never know that she had gone to the funeral. Even though she had been invited and, anyway, Sheila had practically forced her to go.

It was five to seven when Simon's key rattled into the door.

'Here you are!' Pippa cried, hurrying forward, music folder in hand. 'Freddie's watching a cartoon, he's had his tea and he's ready for bed. Ruby's fed and there's a bottle in the fridge for her.'

'Whoa, whoa, whoa!' Simon held his hands up. 'What's the rush?'

'Choir! I'll be late!'

'Ohhh...' He frowned. 'I didn't think you were that bothered.'

'What do you mean? I like it!' Pippa flung her coat on. 'And anyway, they need all the people they can get. It's two weeks till the county heats, you know!'

'I s'pose,' said Simon, noncommittally. 'Drive safe.'

'I will.'

Pippa had to slow herself down several times on the way to the church hall. Not that there were any speed cameras that she knew of, but she'd been cross when someone had screamed past her the other night.

There was a space free in front of the hall, and she eased the Mini into it. Light showed under the door, but Pippa sat for a couple of minutes, psyching herself up, before getting out of the car.

The crowd of people in the hall seemed smaller than usual. 'Hello again, Pippa,' Edie said, advancing with a rueful smile. This week's sweatshirt featured the Powerpuff Girls. 'We're a bit thin on the ground tonight, so thank you for coming.'

'That's fine,' said Pippa, looking for other familiar faces.

'We'll give it a couple more minutes.' Edie resumed her conversation with — was it one of the sopranos? Pippa couldn't keep them straight in her head. People were standing round in twos and threes. She stationed herself on the edge of a group and did a quick headcount. Definitely not as many — maybe three-quarters? Where was everyone? And where was Jen?

It seemed a long two minutes before Edie walked into the centre of the room and clapped her hands. 'Places, everyone. I'm afraid Jen can't make it tonight, so you'll have to put up with me. And my pencil.' She produced a pink, fluffy-ended pencil and waved it in the air. 'Follow this, and as long as we get to the end together we'll all be fine.' She tapped the stand. 'Warm-up!'

As Edie led them through a selection of scales, oohs, ahhs, and eees, Pippa's mind roamed free. Was Jen all right? Edie hadn't said why she wasn't there . . . but it couldn't be anything too bad, as Jen must have asked Edie to fill in. Maybe she was stuck at work — Pippa froze as she realised she was singing alone.

'That's why you need to watch the pencil,' said Edie, her voice kinder than her words. A few giggles and snorts ran through the choir. 'We'll run through the medley. Soloists, stand forward please. I'll do the best I can.'

Pippa watched Edie's fluffy pink pencil like a hawk until break time. She suspected that if the lights had been switched off she would have glowed red. At any rate, she did keep up and sing more bits of the medley, though parts of the transitions remained beyond her. From some of the sounds behind her, she wasn't the only one. There were a few nasty moments, with one particularly teeth-grinding discord, but Edie seemed unfazed, and the pink pencil moved as smoothly and jauntily as ever, ending the piece with a neat little flourish.

'We made it. Just.' She smiled. 'It's hard to sing and lead at the same time, you know. I'll chat with a few of you at break.' The smile had left her eyes when she said those words.

Pippa gulped. She wasn't one of the few, was she? She'd tried really hard, and followed the pencil and everything... Even so, she joined the drinks queue with a thumping heart.

A hand touched her elbow. 'Are you all right?'

It was the mousy woman she had chatted with the previous week. 'Oh, hello... Yes, yes I'm fine. How are you?'

'I've had better days,' the woman said, quietly. 'Were you there this morning?'

'I was, yes.'

The corners of her mouth turned up; no more. 'Sorry, dear. I probably saw you, but people look so different out of their normal clothes. It was quite a good service, I suppose, but —' She waved an incoherent hand. 'We're all over the place.'

They inched nearer to the urn. Out of the corner of her eye Pippa saw Edie walking towards a group of three — were they altos? They were standing in a tight circle, but Edie marched up and inserted herself. 'A word, ladies,' she said, briskly.

'We were having a discussion,' one of them said, turning away from her.

'I'm sure you were,' said Edie. 'We can take the chat outside.'

Another woman snorted. 'Suits me,' she said. 'I could do with a smoke break.'

Edie wrinkled her nose. The door fell to after them, letting in an icy sliver of thin air.

Pippa shuffled forward with the queue, thinking furiously. That second, slightly husky voice — wasn't that...

The voice from the bus shelter?

The cigarette would fit, too.

'The tall woman who just went out,' she said to her

companion, 'what's her name? I think I know her from somewhere.'

'Siobhan, you mean? The one in the red top?'

'That's right,' said Pippa. 'The husky one.'

The mousy woman thought. 'She's a cleaner at the high school. You know, at Gadding Magna.'

'I must be mistaken, then,' said Pippa. 'Mine aren't even at primary school yet.'

'It'll happen before you know it.' She looked quizzically at Pippa. 'I don't know your name.'

'I'm Pippa.'

'Glenys.' Pippa wondered if she ought to shake hands, but Glenys was scanning the queue. 'It seems to be taking forever tonight. Still, it'll give Edie time to have her word.'

Pippa leaned in. 'What do you think she wants to talk about?'

Glenys grimaced. 'Them going deliberately off-key like that. What a crunch! They think they can try it on because Jen's not here, but Edie'll give them what for.'

'Why would they do that?' Pippa asked, as innocently as she possibly could.

'There's history.' Glenys stuck a teabag in a cup and filled it at the urn. 'You?'

'Yes, please. Just milk.'

Glenys handed her the cup and led the way to a quiet corner. 'They were here when we had the previous choirmaster, Des. Lovely man, Des. He was the head music teacher at the high school. He still comes to our concerts, you know.'

'That's nice,' said Pippa, feeling that a contribution, however bland, was required.

'He was very traditional, you see. Fauré's Requiem,

Hallelujah Chorus, everyone standing in place. Then he retired, and Jen took us over, along with his job.'

'Ah.'

'And quite a few people didn't like it. Now me, I've got used to the change. I mean, I wouldn't go out and buy all the stuff we sing —' Glenys wrinkled her nose much as Edie had done. 'But I suppose it's not the same old thing every other year. Anyway.' She counted on her fingers. 'Some people loved it. Some people hated it. Most of those went off to church choirs. The three that have gone with Edie are among the haters, and they're the obstinate sort who throw a spanner in the works every now and then. Some people didn't mind either way. There weren't many of those,' she said, reflectively. 'This sort of thing, it's like Marmite. Most people aren't neutral about it.'

'How did Claire feel about the change?'

'She loved it,' Glenys said quietly. 'She'd enjoyed the choir with Des, but her voice came alive when Jen took over. She really threw herself into it. Of course, Jen is an excellent teacher.'

'I don't see why that group would try to sabotage things, though.' Pippa sipped her tea, which was nuclear-hot. 'If they hate the music that much, why not leave?'

Glenys shrugged. 'They don't approve of Jen, and they like being a thorn in her side. Not usually when it matters, in competitions, or concerts. But they give a little reminder every so often that they could mess things up, if they wanted.'

'Don't approve of what? Her taste in music?' Pippa's voice rose, and she shushed herself hastily.

'Not just that.' Glenys said, looking at the floor. 'Her taste in women.'

'You mean —'

'Claire was a devout Roman Catholic,' Glenys said, and there was steel in her voice. 'She would never have cheated on Pete, never have left him. But yes, Jen, um — liked her. And that's why she isn't here tonight.'

CHAPTER 14

Pippa's brain was far too full to do more than hum along. Luckily much of the second half of the rehearsal was occupied with different sections being taken through the transitions by Edie, meaning that Pippa could let her mind wander. She longed to talk more to Glenys, or to be at home, alone, with a glass of wine, a notepad, and the internet.

Surely no-one would kill Claire to get back at Jen?

Or did Claire feel as if she was in an impossible situation? Was she unable to cope?

Pippa felt dizzy. She was relieved when Edie called time.

'A rehearsal of two halves,' she said drily. 'However, we managed to pull together at the end. Now, Jen gave me a sheet about next week's heats.' She pulled a small square of paper from her pocket and unfolded it, smoothing it out on the stand. 'Next Sunday, half past one, Gadcester Town Hall, back entrance. Dress code as usual.' Her eyes found Pippa. 'Black trousers or black skirt, any length. White top, any style except boob tube or bikini. Black shoes. Hair however you like.'

Pippa decided her suit would get another airing after all, since her ex-maternity pants were scarcely performance wear.

Her phone buzzed in her pocket. *Just a text, not a call.*

It buzzed again. *That would be the repeat.*

She was standing in the second row. She had cover. Her eyes on Edie, Pippa eased the phone from her pocket.

Come home now.

It was from Simon.

Pippa excuse-me'd her way to the end of the row. 'Sorry, urgent message,' she apologised to Edie, whose eyebrows were halfway up her forehead.

'Half one on Sunday, Pippa. Gadcester Town Hall.'

'Yes, yes,' said Pippa, hurrying out.

She started the Mini and tried Simon's mobile. It went straight to voicemail. The house phone rang out, too. Her stomach lurched. What on earth had happened?

It couldn't be an accident, or illness — he'd have said go to the hospital... She put the car into gear and turned carefully out, only remembering to put her lights on when someone flashed theirs at her.

She drove home feeling as if the car might slip out of control at any moment. The car park hadn't felt icy — frosty, if anything. But she could fall off the edge of the world, if she wasn't careful. The knot of tension in her stomach grew bigger, more intricately painful, the closer she got to home.

Simon's car was in the drive. There was no ambulance, no police car. The downstairs lights were on. Pippa parked next to Simon, leaving plenty of room, then walked the plank to the front door.

Simon wasn't watching TV. He was sitting at the dining

table, still in his work clothes, his phone placed square before him. For some reason Pippa thought of a tray of surgical instruments.

'What is it?'

His eyes flicked to the phone, back to her, away again. 'Mum rang,' he said to the table.

Oh God.

'She mentioned that she went to her friend's daughter's funeral today. With you.'

'She asked me to!'

'Why didn't you tell me, then?' He paused, briefly. 'Because you knew I wouldn't want you to go, and that I'd try and stop you. And you'd have been right.'

'If you're going to answer questions for me, there's no point me staying here —' Pippa turned to go, but the scrape of Simon's chair on the wooden floor stopped her dead.

'Don't you dare, Pippa.' Simon's palms were flat on the table, his arms wide, his face black as thunder. He seemed ready to launch himself across the table at her. But slowly his jaw unclenched a little, and he sat down.

'Sit.'

She obeyed.

'This stops now, Pippa. This sneaking behind my back, insinuating yourself into places where you *just shouldn't be*...' Simon pushed his hair off his forehead and fixed the table with a hard stare. 'It sickens me,' he said quietly.

Pippa could feel tears prickling. 'Don't you care that someone might have been killed?'

'No one has been killed,' he said, wearily. 'Someone has, unfortunately and tragically, died. No-one will appreciate you poking around in the wreckage of that poor woman's life!' He smacked the table, hard, and Pippa felt it like a punch in the gut.

It was no good. The tears poured out of her. She laid her head on her arms and sobbed.

'Crying won't win me round,' Simon said, savagely. But after a minute or two he came round the table. 'Come on,' he said, putting a hand on her shoulder. 'Stop that.'

Pippa lifted her head up and stared at him. 'I can't stop!' she cried. 'I didn't ask for this to happen! I just went to choir, like a normal person, and the next thing I know someone's died! The choir's split in two — people are whispering in corners — her husband was looking at someone at the funeral in an odd way — a woman sneaked out of the church and hurried off, and tonight I heard — oh never mind.' Her cheek was burning hot as she laid it against the cool wood of the table.

'Take it to the police, Pip.' Simon stroked her hair. 'If you're really worried. I'm sorry I shouted.' He exhaled, sharply. 'Mum was gossiping about the funeral and I nearly lost my rag with her. You probably got the tail end of that.' He got up. 'I'll make a brew. But I mean it. Go to the police. Apart from anything else, do you think it's a good idea to let people know what you're doing when there's a potential murderer on the loose?'

'I wouldn't let people know!' Pippa's voice quietened as Simon raised his eyebrows at her. 'All right. I'll go to the station tomorrow and talk to PC Horsley. I can ask Lila to mind Freddie at playgroup.'

'Good.' Simon stood up, giving her a final pat. 'I'll get the kettle on.'

As the kettle stuttered into life Pippa fetched a notepad and pen, and turned to a fresh page.

Murder?, she wrote.

Claire — what was her last name? Staunton, she seemed to recall from the service. She picked up her phone and typed *Gadding Messenger Claire Staunton obit.*

The details flashed up, with Claire's photo.

Claire Staunton, forty-six, married with two teenage children. Husband, Pete, surveyor, works away a lot. Volunteered at the Gadcester Hospice Shop in Gadding Magna. How long had she worked there?

Gadding Magna. Where the high school was. Where Jen taught music.

The kettle pinged.

Breathless. Used a spray (what sort? Is it a GTN spray?). Died of a heart attack. Maybe angina? Did she use the spray on the night she died? Could she have been given something to make a heart attack more likely? Or did someone take her spray?

Doctor's records. Was a doctor called, or a paramedic?

Who was Pete looking at in the congregation?

Who was that young woman in black? Where was she going? Would Sheila know?

Pippa's pen skittered across the page as Simon coughed. 'Aren't you handing this one over to the cops?' he asked, as he put Pippa's Buffy the Vampire Slayer mug on a coaster and slid it towards her.

'I am.' Pippa let the pen drop. 'I'm making notes so that I remember it all.'

'Mm.' But Simon didn't look convinced.

***

Pippa woke surprisingly well-rested. She had expected to toss and turn on the horns of a moral dilemma, but

Simon had had to wake her for both of Ruby's feeds. Perhaps that was the effect of washing her hands of the problem. And if so, then clearly it was the right thing to do.

She texted Lila after breakfast. *Will you be at playgroup? If so could you watch F for me? Thanks P x*

A response by return. *Yes till 11. Why? L x*

Pippa sighed. *Tell you later. Maybe x.* She wasn't sure that she would. She shoved the notepad into her changing bag and tried to focus on getting the children and herself ready. Even so, she had to check the changing bag three times before she was sure everything was there. Everything felt — scattered.

She was at playgroup ten minutes early, and began getting the toys out as a distraction. What if PC Horsley was on patrol, or at a meeting?

'I thought it was my turn today,' said Eva, walking in with a puzzled look on her face. 'I'm not late, am I?'

'No, no,' said Pippa, 'I was just here and . . . it keeps Freddie busy.'

'True,' said Eva. 'Let me give you a hand with that.' She took the other end of the play kitchen and together they manoeuvred it easily out of the cupboard. 'There.' She brushed her hands together and went to fetch more toys.

Lila appeared at two minutes to ten. Not that Pippa was checking the time. 'Hey,' she said. 'Off you go, then.'

'Thanks, Lila.' Pippa bent and kissed Freddie on the forehead. 'Mummy has to pop out for a bit. Ask Aunty Lila if you need anything.'

Freddie nodded solemnly, turning a toy car over in his hands.

Pippa wheeled Ruby out of the church hall, past St Saviour's and round the corner to the tiny pebbledashed cube which was Much Gadding's police station. She could see lights within. *Yes!*

The door swung open. 'Hello?' called Pippa, backing the pushchair in.

There was a slight flurry behind the counter, which sounded like the hasty folding of a newspaper, then PC Horsley stood up. 'Hello, Mrs Parker. What can I do for you today?' His eyes fell to the pushchair. 'No Freddie?'

'He's at playgroup.' Now that she was here, Pippa wasn't sure how to begin.

PC Horsley raised an eyebrow. 'I take it this isn't a social call.'

'Good God, no.'

PC Horsley waited, conspicuously.

'Can we go into the back room?' Pippa gabbled.

PC Horsley's other eyebrow went up. 'I take it this isn't an everyday matter.'

Pippa shook her head. 'No. I'm — not sure.'

PC Horsley took a key from its hook on the wall and locked the main door. 'You'd better come through, then.'

PC Horsley placed a chair for Pippa, then bent to offer Ruby a finger. 'She's grown, hasn't she?'

'Um, yes.' Pippa sat down and looked at her daughter.

'How old is she now? Six months?'

'More like three.' Pippa smiled. 'I thought you'd have remembered.'

The policeman snorted. 'Thought I'd be delivering her. Is it really three months?' He gently released Ruby's grip, then took a seat opposite Pippa. 'So. What brings you here, Mrs Parker?'

'It's —' Pippa rummaged for her notepad. 'I could be wrong, and this isn't official, well, certainly not yet, and maybe not ever —'

The policeman leaned forward. 'Just tell me.'

'Claire Staunton's death. I think it might have been murder.'

PC Horsley's eyebrows climbed again. 'You don't sound very sure.'

'I'm not.'

Gradually, slowly, bit by bit, with lots of questions from PC Horsley, Pippa laid out what she knew, and what she suspected. PC Horsley's face remained as impassive as a statue throughout.

'So it could be a murder, it might be a suicide, but I don't think that Claire died a natural death.' There, she'd said it. She'd done what Simon had asked her to, and laid it in the hands of the police. Pippa looked up at PC Horsley, and waited for a verdict.

The policeman studied the desk for some time. 'Mrs Parker,' he said. His tone was brisk, matter-of-fact. 'You helped us a great deal with the Barbara Hamilton case. There, we definitely had a murder on our hands. No doubt about it. This, however —' He gazed at the *Fugitive* film poster on the wall. 'I can't act on hunches and feelings. If I took this to the Inspector he'd laugh me out of his office.' His gaze was opaque. 'I'm sorry. With nothing concrete, there's nothing I can do. I certainly wouldn't go digging the body up on a hunch.'

'I didn't say that —'

'Then how will you prove it?' His response was quick, but PC Horsley's voice was not aggressive, not challenging. He was reasoning with her.

'I can't,' said Pippa. She had a terrible urge to cry. 'Thank you for your time.' She got up. 'Come on Ruby, back to playgroup.'

PC Horsley held the door for her, silently. Before he opened the main door he looked at her, and there was something in that look that worried her. 'Are you sure you're all right, Mrs Parker?'

'Yes, fine,' said Pippa. She wanted to get out of there. Preferably to sit on her own and cry, but playgroup would have to do.

PC Horsley opened the door. 'All right, then.' She wheeled Ruby away, and as she turned onto the road, glanced back. He was still watching her.

Am I all right? Or am I imagining things?

And now she recognised the emotion on PC Horsley's face when he had looked at her.

Concern.

CHAPTER 15

Pippa checked her watch before opening the door of the church hall. 10:32. The time in the police station had seemed much longer. It was a half-hour she never wished to repeat.

'Pippa!' She turned and Serendipity was standing on the pavement, half hidden behind Monty.

'Oh, hello,' said Pippa, backing the pushchair through the door.

'What are you doing?' Serendipity asked. 'Is it a class?'

'Playgroup,' said Pippa, hoping Serendipity would take the hint. She wasn't in the mood for chatting.

'Oh, can I see? I'll keep Monty under control, don't worry. He's good with children.'

'I suppose,' said Pippa, and Serendipity hurried to grab the door.

The children who could walk, or crawl, crowded round Monty, who lapped up the attention, while several of the adults focused on his owner. 'I had no idea you lived here!' exclaimed Sam, taking the nearest chair. 'I love all your videos!'

'Um, thank you,' said Serendipity, looking round the

hall. 'This is a nice space. I've just moved in, really, so I'm getting to know the village.'

'You could do crafting sessions here,' Sam said. 'Or teach a class. I'd come.'

I bet you would, thought Pippa, unbuckling Ruby and carrying her to the playmat for tummy time. She looked for a chair, but the only unoccupied ones were at the far end of the room.

'Are you going to stay in Much Gadding, do you think?' Sam asked.

'I'm not sure,' said Serendipity. She tucked a strand of hair behind her ear and patted Monty.

'You should,' said Sam. 'You could film a series. Or write a book, and use the village for photos.'

Pippa walked across to Lila, who, for once, did not have her phone in her hand. 'How's Freddie?'

'Absolutely fine.' Lila pointed to where Freddie and Dylan, aided by Henry, were presiding over an obstacle race. 'Busy running the show.' She beckoned to Pippa. 'Where've you been?'

'Something and nothing,' said Pippa, as casually as she could.

''K,' said Lila. 'Tell me later, if you want. Or text.'

'Mm.' Pippa straightened up, met the narrowed eyes of Sam, and looked quickly away. 'I'll go and get a chair,' she said, to no-one in particular.

'Plotting again, Pippa?' said Sam, with a smile that could curdle milk.

'Nope.' Pippa kept walking.

'Pippa's our local Miss Marple,' Sam explained, presumably for Serendipity's benefit. 'Always sniffing things out.'

Pippa selected a chair from the row of identical orange plastic ones, and gripped it tightly.

'Yes, I read about it in the paper,' said Serendipity. 'You solved a murder, didn't you?'

'Yes.' Pippa carried the chair over. 'That was some months ago. Water under the bridge.' She positioned the chair at the edge of the group.

'Everyone needs a hobby, though,' said Sam, grinning. 'I like making jewellery, you like snooping.'

'I do not like snooping!' Pippa cried. 'And I have a hobby, thank you. I belong to a choir.'

'Oh, I love singing!' said Serendipity, most enthusiastically. 'Which choir do you go to? Is it in the village?'

Pippa could have sighed with relief. 'It's in Lower Gadding. They're called Sweet Harmony. I haven't actually been going that long. It's — nice. Lots of variety.'

Sam frowned. 'Sweet Harmony? Where have I heard that lately?'

Pippa allowed herself a moment of smugness. 'We were in the paper. We're competing in the county heats for SingFest UK next weekend.'

'No,' Sam said, thoughtfully. 'Not that.'

Pippa turned to Serendipity. 'Are you settled in at Rosebud Cottage?'

'I think so.' Serendipity looped Monty's lead in her hands. 'But there's always something to do. Homemaking never sleeps.'

'I remember.' Sam's face changed. 'It was in the paper. The woman who died of a heart attack a couple of weeks ago, Claire whatshername. She was a member of Sweet Harmony.' She turned a triumphant beam on Pippa. 'And you've just joined. What a coincidence.'

All the adults' faces turned from Sam to Pippa, as if they were at a tennis match. 'I joined before it happened,' Pippa said stiffly. 'You can ask the choir leader if you don't believe me.' She could feel heat creeping up her neck, and hoped it wasn't visible.

'Mm.' Sam had a look of utter relish on her face. 'I've remembered something else. Wasn't her funeral yesterday?'

Pippa shrugged. 'Yes.'

'And when you came to pick Freddie up from preschool you had a black suit on.' Sam turned to the group in general. 'Like I said, snooping.'

'Shut up, Sam,' snapped Pippa. 'The whole choir was invited.' But she saw everyone's thoughts in their faces.

Serendipity got up. 'Um, I think Monty needs more of a walk. I'll catch you later,' she gabbled, and made a hasty exit.

Sam watched her go, then turned back to Pippa. 'Had you even spoken to the woman who died?' she demanded. 'Before you started ferreting around?'

Pippa's rage boiled over. 'Get out!' she shouted.

Sam stared at her.

'I mean it. Get out.' Pippa stood up and jerked her thumb at the door. 'Take Livvy, and go.'

She felt a touch on her arm. Lila looked genuinely worried. 'Pippa, this isn't —'

'No!' She shook the hand off. 'Every time she speaks to me there's a dig, or a slight, or an — an insinuation, and I've had enough of it.' She turned to Sam, who was still in her chair. 'I can't avoid seeing you in the village, but I don't have to speak to you, and I certainly don't have to put up with you here.'

Sam leaned back in her chair, very deliberately. 'What are you going to do, drag me out?'

'Don't tempt me.' Pippa smiled. 'No, I wouldn't lay a finger on you. But if you don't move your bottom from that chair, I'll close the playgroup. No-one wants that, do they?' She paused. 'Do they?'

An uncomfortable rumble in the negative, and some shaking of heads.

'Fine.' Sam stood up. 'I'll leave you to it. Hope you enjoy yourselves in the new dictatorship.' She bent, scooped Livvy up, ignoring her protests, and carried her out. The door banged behind them.

Pippa sat down before her legs gave way. Her head was spinning. It felt as if her skull was straining to burst through. She put her hands to her forehead to hold it in.

'Pippa?' Lila shook her gently.

'Sorry,' Pippa muttered. 'I was just so angry.'

'I gathered.' Lila held out a hand. 'Come on, I'm taking you home.'

Pippa raised her head. 'It's Thursday. What about your job?'

Lila glanced at her watch, then held her hand out again. 'It'll be fine,' she said quietly. 'Come along, Pippa.'

Pippa ignored the hand and stood up on her own, then went to fetch Ruby. She could feel silent eyes on her as she strapped Ruby in. Judging eyes, no doubt.

Lila was waiting by the door, holding Bella and Freddie's hands. Both children looked confused.

'Is Mummy ill?' Freddie asked.

'Time to go home, Freddie,' said Lila.

'But —'

'Come on.' She opened the door and took his hand again. 'You like riding in my car, don't you?'

'Yay!' shouted Freddie, everything else forgotten.

Pippa tried to help Lila fold the pushchair, find the spare seat and strap in the children, but Lila shooed her off.

'You can just drop us, you know,' she said, as the overloaded Fiat chugged past the village green.

'No,' said Lila.

She parked outside Pippa's house a few minutes later. 'Let's get you in.'

'I'm not an invalid.' Pippa unbuckled her seatbelt, which shot back into its holder.

'No. But you look awful.'

'Thanks.' Pippa opened her door and fumbled in the changing bag for her keys. Her hand brushed the notepad, and she wanted to scream.

At least the house was tidy. Lila followed Pippa into the house, went to the kitchen, and flicked the kettle on.

'I'm fine. Honest.'

Lila lined up two mugs. 'You make tea, then. I'll go and put the TV on for the kids.'

Pippa sighed and reached for the teabags. Presently the TV came on, and loud jingles followed. 'That'll hold them,' said Lila. 'I'll do juice and biscuits in a minute.'

'You can still —'

'I'm not leaving you alone,' Lila said flatly. The kettle pinged and she poured water into the mugs. 'What was all that about?' she said, softly.

'It really did happen after I'd joined the choir,' said Pippa, her eyes on the mugs. 'And the whole choir was invited to the funeral.'

'But you do think something's wrong, don't you?'

'Yes,' Pippa admitted. 'I'm not sure what, and I didn't even know her, but — you know when you just feel something's a bit off?'

Lila nodded.

'I didn't want to — I don't want to get involved.' Pippa pushed her fringe back. 'But I keep — noticing things. It's calling me, somehow. And no-one else will help me. Simon told me I should hand it over to the police. I tried this morning, and PC Horsley said he couldn't do anything.'

'I'll help you.' Lila found a teaspoon and scooped the teabags out, flicking them into the bin. 'Not sure how, mind. But I knew something was up.' She looked up at Pippa. 'I wondered if you might have post-natal depression.'

Pippa turned the idea over in her mind. 'I don't think so,' she said. 'I'm bored, and frustrated. And tired, of course. But that's normal with a new baby, isn't it? Oh, and freaked out about turning thirty.'

'It isn't that bad,' said Lila. 'I just got drunk.'

'Thanks for the life advice.' Pippa grinned. 'It helps that you don't think I'm a fantasist or a coffin-chaser. God knows about the rest of the playgroup.'

'Sam's a cow.' Lila fetched the milk. 'I don't know why she's got her claws into you, but she's known for it. She pecks away at people. Strong or weak?'

It took a second for Pippa to realise that Lila meant the tea. 'Strong, please.'

'She'll probably bother someone else now. Cheers.' Lila raised her mug and Pippa clinked it. 'Do you think you'll let her back into playgroup?'

'I'll see how I feel.' Pippa mused. 'If she apologises,

maybe.'

'Don't hold your breath.' Lila blew on her tea, then slurped. 'You know what you need?'

'Another pair of hands? Forty-eight hours in the day? An invisibility cloak?'

'Close.' Lila grinned. 'You need an assistant. Another pair of eyes and ears to do some of the legwork. Hastings to your Poirot, Watson to your Holmes.'

Pippa goggled. 'Are you volunteering?'

'Me? God, no!' Lila giggled. 'I'd be awful. I'd go up to suspects and poke them and be all "It was you, wasn't it? Spill!"'

'Maybe not, then.' Pippa found herself giggling too. She couldn't remember the last time she'd laughed properly. 'But who?'

'What about Norm in the library?' said Lila. 'He was a policeman, he knows the drill.'

Pippa shook her head. 'He's already said no.'

'Darn.' Suddenly Lila's face brightened. 'OK. Imagine you're recruiting someone. What qualities do they need?'

Pippa considered. 'Well, they need to be inquisitive. The sort of person who notices things. Preferably someone who isn't constantly distracted by small children. Oh, and who doesn't work, so they come and go as they please. They know a lot of people in the area, so they can get information —'

'There you are,' said Lila. 'The ideal candidate, hiding in plain sight.'

'What? Who?'

Lila grinned. 'I can't believe you haven't worked it out. Call yourself a detective!'

'Lila! Who?'

Lila sipped her tea and regarded Pippa teasingly over the rim of her mug. 'Who do you complain about most? Who winds you up with their constant busybodying and gossiping?'

'Oh my gosh.' Pippa put her mug down. 'I'm an idiot.'

Lila drained her mug and put it on the worktop. 'You look a hundred times better already. Can I leave you to get on with that line of enquiry? I have a child to drop off and a plausible excuse to invent.'

'Go for it. And thank you.'

Lila regarded her steadily. 'You saved my bacon when the cops suspected me of killing Barbara. If I can help, I will. Always.' She encircled Pippa in a brief, brisk hug, then stomped out. 'Bella! Time to dash!'

Pippa peeped into the sitting room. Freddie was glued to a cartoon. Ruby was asleep in her car seat. She might have as much as ten minutes' free time. She crept into the kitchen, and pulled out her phone.

New Message

Her fingers flew over the keyboard. *Would you like to come for coffee on Monday morning? I have an idea, and I think you'd be interested. Can't talk in front of Freddie. Top secret.*

That should do it. Pippa clicked on the *To* field, and scrolled through her contacts.

Sheila.

Send.

CHAPTER 16

Pippa looked doubtfully up at the town hall. It loomed much more menacingly than she remembered. Why had she thought joining a choir was a good idea?

'You'll be fine.' Edie was surprisingly smart in black and white, without a cartoon character in sight. 'Sorry, didn't mean to make you jump. Come on, we'd better go in. It's almost half one.'

Pippa's nerves diminished a little as they walked down an alley to a small, peeling back door. Edie led the way into a dim passage, adorned with a sign scrawled in blue marker pen: *SingFest UK heats THIS WAY*.

'Here we go.' Edie opened a door labelled *CHOIRS* on a sheet of A4, and they stepped inside.

It was mayhem. Crowds and crowds of people, some of them children, dressed in their different choir uniforms, chatting, singing, practising moves. Pippa had assumed they would have their own dressing room, where they would chat politely and wait to be called. She blinked, but the wall of noise was still there.

'Over here!' Jen waved both arms in the air, and Pippa followed Edie through the jungle of performers. 'Good, I can mark you off.' She picked up a clipboard and ticked twice. 'Three more to come. Has anyone spoken to Eileen?'

'She definitely said she was coming,' said one of the sopranos.

'Mmm.' Jen added a question mark to her sheet. 'Dave's wife rang and said he had the flu, so —' She drew a savage line through Dave. 'Siobhan?'

Everyone looked blank. 'We'll have to see, then.' Jen added another question mark.

'Right you lot, listen up. The good news is that we're the first choir on. That means we get it done, we hear the other choirs, and also, if anyone needs to sneak off, they can. The bad news is that I don't think the choir who goes on first has ever won the Gadcestershire heat of SingFest. But the top three choirs go through to the regional heats anyway, so hey, it isn't a disaster.' She paused, and the smile vanished from her face. 'I'm sorry I missed our last rehearsal. But whatever our personal feelings, let's sing up and make this our best performance. For Claire.'

'For Claire,' the choir echoed, heads bowed.

'Ten minutes!' yelled a voice. 'Sweet Harmony, come to ME, please.'

Pippa shuffled forward obediently in the crowd of black and white sheep until she saw a young woman with a headset, standing on a box. 'OK! Follow me to the stage.' She jumped down and the sheep filtered out of Babel, along another narrow corridor. 'Places, please.'

Pippa couldn't see anything for the crowd. Gradually, though, it thinned as people moved forward and organised themselves into sections. She progressed down the dark passage, then gasped.

She was in the wings, and before her was a stage. A big stage. The only thing which made it less frightening was that the curtain was closed. Pippa imagined the seats beyond, and the people in them, and shuddered. But she couldn't stop now. For one thing, she had no idea how to get out of this place. She walked forward, and inserted herself next to Edie.

The young woman clapped her hands. 'OK! This is how it works! We're due to start in five minutes.' She held up her spread hand to emphasise the point. 'The compere will be in front of the curtain. He'll talk for a few minutes, get the crowd worked up, then the curtain rises on you lot. You do your thing, take the applause, curtain down, you go off, next lot on. Clear?'

Nods and murmurs. At least the torture would be short. And Simon wouldn't be there. He had made vague noises about coming, which she had deflected with speed and enthusiasm. 'You'll put me off. Plus the kids would never put up with however many hours of singing.' Her jaw dropped as she realised a further horror. 'Freddie might sing along!'

'OK, OK!' Simon shrugged. 'I was trying to be supportive.'

'I know,' said Pippa. 'Let's just leave it as a nice thought.'

She stood hastily to attention as Jen rapped her baton on the music stand. 'You know what to do. Soloists, get yourselves where you can step out easily.' Cue shuffling. Pippa tried not to let her face fall as Edie moved forward. 'Three things. Follow me. Follow your section leaders. And don't forget to smile. You are supposed to be enjoying it, you know.' Jen scanned the choir. 'That's a bit better.

Good luck, everyone.' She turned towards the curtain as the speakers blared.

'Welcome to the Gadcestershire heats of SingFest UK 2017! And here's your host, Gadcester FM DJ Riiiiiiitz Robertsonnnn!'

Applause broke out in the hall. Ritz Robertson, presumably, had arrived on stage.

His disembodied voice boomed. 'Hello Gadcester!'

Cheers and whoops from the audience.

'Who likes a sing-song?'

'We do!' the audience shouted.

'And we have some wonderful singers for you today! But first, let me introduce our judges! Professor of Music at the University of Gadcestershire, Tony Kendall! Newspaper columnist for the *Gadcester Chronicle*, Janey Dixon! And last but not least, noted pantomime dame Chilly Winters!'

The crowd roared. Pippa blinked. *Bloody Janey Dixon. Put-ten-years-on-me Janey Dixon. Still, at least she won't know who I am, and I can get a look at her. Bet she isn't twenty-nine.*

'Right, settle down you lot or we'll never get started! And our first choir is the very talented Sweet Harmony, a community choir from Lower Gadding. Give 'em a big hand!'

The crowd obliged, and the curtain rose. Ritz Robertson, a balding man in a tight pink suit, waved at them, then ran offstage. Jen blew her pitchpipe and raised her baton. *One-two-three-four!*

The time flew. There was so much to do — watching Jen, listening for Edie, keeping up, remembering to breathe (and, of course, smile), that it seemed like seconds until

Jen's baton flourished the end. She grinned broadly and mouthed 'Best one yet,' as the audience clapped and whistled.

Pippa felt dazed. She couldn't believe it was over.

'Weren't they good?' Ritz Robertson said, applauding as he walked back on, and the curtain fell.

The young woman ran from the wings and shooed them down the passage. 'Quick! The next group are waiting!' she hissed. Their feet were ridiculously loud on the wooden stage, but it didn't matter. Ritz Robertson was working the crowd, and any noise they were making was completely drowned.

Pippa emerged into the corridor, where a line of well-scrubbed children waited patiently. Ah, the cute factor at work. Red ribbons in the girls' hair, red bow ties and braces for the boys. Pippa made a mental note to ask Jen whether they should consider a slightly more showy stage outfit.

'This way!' Jen shouted, and they went left instead of right. 'We'll go and listen now. You can leave whenever you want, so long as you don't go in the middle of an act. Bad karma.'

A few people peeled off, muttering about getting back for the football or making a start on the ironing. Pippa knew that she had a million and one things which she could be getting on with, but her feet followed Jen to the door marked *Auditorium*. The children were piping away, and Jen waited for the applause before pushing the door open. 'Our block is over here.'

Their block turned out to be a set of wooden chairs beside the main seating. Pippa sat down between Glenys and one of the tenors — was it Ray? — and surveyed the scene. The judges were sitting behind a table, and seemed to be conferring. How had she not seen that one of them was in full panto dame rig? Chilly Winters, presumably. A man with longish grey hair and a black leather jacket sat in the middle — the music professor? And next to him, a sharp-nosed woman with frizzy blonde hair and blood-red lipstick. Janey Dixon.

The curtain dropped; the shouty young woman would be herding the children off. 'Wonder who's on next,' Ray said, stretching his legs out.

He didn't have to wonder long. 'Our next group of singers is small,' Ritz Robertson brought his hands together, 'but perfectly formed.' He tiptoed to the curtain and peeked through, closing it and doubling up in ostentatious laughter. 'Wait till you see what they've got back there! Tony!'

The professor raised his head inquiringly.

Ritz Robertson leaned forward confidentially. 'I think you'll like this lot. You've got something in common.' He straightened up and addressed the room. 'Are you ready for Short Back and Sides?'

'Yes!' the audience shouted happily.

'I didn't hear you! Are you ready?'

'YES!' they roared.

'All right then! Give it up for Short Back And Siiiiiiiides!'

The curtain rose and a horn blasted.

A motorbike horn.

There was a large, shiny silver motorbike in the middle of the stage. Various men, all in jeans and leather jackets, were loafing around it. One man, jacketless, straddled the bike. He wore a tight white T-shirt, and his hair was a high black quiff.

Where was their conductor?

T-Shirt Man swung his leg over the bike, stood up, and tapped his foot. *One-two-three-four.* And they burst into 'Leader Of The Pack'.

Pippa blinked. There were, what, twenty or so men on the stage, and they seemed to be singing twenty different parts with absolute precision. They must have got their note from the motorbike horn. She shook her head in disbelief.

'These are the ones to beat,' Ray muttered. 'They're practically semi-pro. They do small venues round the county. Oh my gosh.' His eyes widened.

Pippa looked back to the stage. T-Shirt Man was now sitting on the bike, the rest of the choir behind him, and the music had somehow shifted into — was that an Ed Sheeran song? He was solo, with the others providing backing, and the music seemed to flow out of him. Suddenly he dismounted and began to walk forward, still singing, and the others fell into step. They must be getting ready to go into their final song.

Pippa frowned, and sat up to get an uninterrupted view.

T-Shirt Man's profile showed clearly against the dark wings. Pippa watched him as the volume grew, the pace slowed, and the group modulated into — what else — 'Greased Lightning'. They were standing in a line, pointing out into the audience. People were stamping their feet to the beat.

The group moved into the final chord, raising their arms, and ended clean as a whistle.

The audience leapt to their feet. Pippa found herself rising too. The group were grinning, taking the applause, waving to the crowd, except for T-Shirt Man, who seemed sheepish, as if he'd somehow been talked into the whole thing.

And then Pippa was absolutely sure.

It was Jeff.

CHAPTER 17

'I'm just popping to the toilet,' Pippa muttered, sidling down her row and making for the door they had come in by. She had a pretty good idea that that was not the way to the toilet. Then again, she wasn't sure how to reach backstage, either. But everyone was too busy clapping and commenting to worry about what she was doing. The curtain fell and Ritz Robertson bounded on stage. *I have to be quick.*

Pippa hurried down the corridor, listening for clues. There were two paths she could take at the end — Aha! Excited male voices, coming from her right. She paused out of sight, and waited.

Leather jackets passed, their owners grinning and euphoric.

'We couldn't have done it better!'

'I reckon it's in the bag!'

'Boom!'

'Awesome!'

As she had expected, her quarry was bringing up the rear. She peeped round the corner and almost bumped into him.

'Oh, sorry, I didn't see you —'

'Hello, Jeff.'

He did a perfect double take and stared at her. Pippa couldn't tell if he was wearing contact lenses, or if he genuinely didn't recognise her.

'Pippa. Lila's friend. We met at the Rambler's Rest.'

She could see his mind flicking through options. 'I think you're mistaken,' he said, finally. 'My name isn't Jeff.'

'Come off it, Clark Kent.' He winced. 'So . . . is this the hobby you won't tell Lila about?'

He studied his feet.

'Why not?'

Jeff backed away a little. 'I, um, I don't want to.'

'But you were really good.' Pippa smiled encouragingly at him. 'Seriously good.'

'That's not the point,' he muttered.

'What is, then?'

'Look, this is *my* thing, and I keep it separate from everything else. My colleagues at the bank don't know I sing. My parents don't know I sing. My choir friends don't know where I work. They don't know my last name, even. I'm just a guy who sings.'

'Who yer talking to, Jeff?' A leather jacket was standing in the corridor.

'Be there in a minute,' Jeff replied.

Pippa watched Leather Jacket disappear. 'When will you tell Lila?'

'When I'm ready,' said Jeff.

'And will that be this century? She'll worm it out of you, you know. She hates secrets.'

Jeff's mouth turned down. 'I gathered,' he said quietly. 'I know her that well, you see.' He sighed. 'It's just —'

'I don't think she'd mind. In fact...' Pippa hesitated, then ploughed on. 'She might like it.'

'*Like* it?' Jeff sounded incredulous.

'Yes.' Pippa found it hard to reconcile this timid, reluctant man with the confident performer she had seen minutes earlier. 'You, singing, centre stage. I think she would like to see you, um, strutting your stuff.'

Jeff shuddered. 'It's too soon.'

'You do realise,' Pippa said, blandly, 'that if Sweet Harmony gets through to the regional competition Lila will probably come. And you lot are a shoo-in.'

'Oh God.' Jeff ran his hand through his quiff, bringing the front part down. 'I mean, I don't want your choir not to go through, but —' He raised his hands. 'Give me time, OK?' And he scurried away. Even his back looked defensive.

Pippa made her way slowly to the auditorium. Poor Jeff. Although how he'd managed to keep it quiet... She opened the door, heard singing, and hastily pulled it shut. From the sound of this one, they wouldn't be going any further. The tenors were well off the beat.

Had Sweet Harmony done enough to reach the regional final? She couldn't tell. But there hadn't been any errors. No rogue altos today. Was Siobhan's absence deliberate, and if it was, what had Edie said to her after the last rehearsal? She considered asking Edie, but shrank from the thought. Edie would tell her to mind her own business. And she would probably be justified.

Polite applause, and Pippa made her way back to her seat.

'You didn't miss much,' said Ray, giving the side-eye to the stage.

'One more choir!' declared Ritz Robertson, leaping into view. 'Then the judges will decide, and announce the REGIONAL FINALISTS of SingFest UK!'

'Wooooooooo!' cooed the crowd, obediently.

The last group was a church choir, resplendent in surplices, who were skilled but static, and uncomfortable on the stage. They sang, smiled queasily at their applause, and Pippa spied at least two grateful expressions as the curtain came down.

'And there you have it! Five fabulous choirs, but only three can go through to the regional heats.' Ritz Robertson shaded his eyes and peered into the auditorium. 'Head judge Tony, how long will it take to reach a result?'

The judges conferred. 'Minutes,' said the professor.

'Jolly good. Talk amongst yourselves then, members of the audience. No peeking at the scoresheets!' The DJ wagged a finger.

'I can't abide that man,' Glenys muttered. 'It's like being at a holiday camp.'

'Do you think we'll get through?' Pippa whispered.

'It'll be the first time if we do,' Glenys whispered back. 'It would be wonderful, though.' Her eyes were shining.

Light muzak came through the PA system. 'Where is the regional final?' Pippa asked.

'They hold it at Danbrook Spa,' breathed Glenys. 'In the Great Hall.'

'Ooh, lovely.' Pippa had never visited Danbrook Spa, but she assumed it would have Georgian buildings and an air of stuffy gentility.

'Ladies and gentlemen!' Ritz Robertson was onstage again, grinning in a slightly demonic manner. 'We have a result! Head judge Tony, please join me on the stage.'

The professor walked slowly up the steps. He reminded Pippa of an elderly dinosaur in need of a nap. The microphone squealed as he adjusted it upwards. 'Sorry about that,' he muttered. 'These are the choirs who have reached the regional final. As is traditional, they are in reverse order.' He allowed himself a wintry smile.

'In third place, Sweet Harmony.'

'We're going! We're going!' shrieked Glenys, and threw her arms round Pippa.

The judge was looking their way and speaking, but it was drowned out by their squeals and cheers and exclamations. Pippa could hear giggles from the audience. Tony Kendall waited until the noise had subsided to a reasonable level before continuing.

'In second place, Kids Aloud.'

A high-pitched eruption from the right-hand side of the room, and several sets of red flashes jumping up and down.

'And finally — and I don't think this will surprise anyone — first place goes to Short Back and Sides.'

The audience cheered and stamped.

'What a result!' beamed Ritz Robertson, moving Tony Kendall out of the way to get to the microphone. 'Sweet Harmony, third prize winners, please come to the stage!'

They dutifully trooped up and stood there while the judges shook hands with Jen and presented her with a small plastic shield. Photographs were taken, and they were hustled back down.

'Kids Aloud, come on up for your moment of fame!'

The children invaded the stage, talking excitedly to each other. It was all the photographers could do to get them to stand still for a picture with Chilly Winters.

'And finally, Short Back and Sides, winners of the Gadcestershire heat of SingFeeeeeeeest!' Ritz Robertson pointed a playful finger. 'Now don't bring that motorbike back on!'

A small army of leather jackets ascended the steps. *Where was Jeff? Surely he hadn't left?* Pippa felt a pang of guilt. What if he'd missed his big moment because she had rattled him so much? But no, there was a black quiff, slightly above the rest. Tony Kendall advanced, looking slightly confused until one of the others pointed to Jeff, and then he beamed and pumped Jeff's hand. Jeff's expression changed from utter embarrassment to a shy smile, and he cracked a grin when Tony presented him with the trophy, a medium-sized gold cup. Pippa wondered if the trophies for the next round would be any better. Still, it was the winning that counted, wasn't it? The photographers advanced, and Jeff immediately stepped behind someone else. But it was no use. One of the photographers shouted 'Let's have one with the bike!' It was wheeled on stage and the choir draped themselves over it. 'Get that trophy in shot!'

Jeff tried to hand it to one of his colleagues, who promptly pushed it back at him. 'No you don't!' he shouted. 'On yer bike, Jeff!'

To his credit, Jeff didn't run. He got on the bike and posed obediently.

'Hold the trophy up higher!' called a photographer. 'It's in front of your face!'

Jeff did as he was told, and held a rigid grin while they snapped. Pippa felt for him. But eventually the photographers lowered their cameras and the choir loped off, with much high-fiving and back-slapping.

'And that's it for another year of SingFest UK in Gadcester Town Hall!' cried Ritz Robertson, sweating in his pink suit. 'You've been a lovely audience, let's do it again next year. I've been Ritz Robertson, and you can catch me on Gadcester FM's breakfast show, six till nine weekdays. Over and out!' He bounced off stage, and the muzak started up.

'They deserved it, didn't they,' Pippa said to Glenys.

Glenys looked startled. 'Who? I'm sorry, I was miles away.'

'Short Back And Sides. They deserved to win.'

'Oh.' Glenys wrinkled her nose. 'Them. If you like that sort of boyband thing.'

'I take it you don't.'

Glenys snorted. 'Crowd-pleasing rubbish. Oh, I don't deny that they sing it well,' she said. 'But it's not proper music, is it?' She sighed. 'I thought the church choir would have done better. But there you go, pop music wins again.'

'Hang on,' said Pippa. 'By your definition, most of what we sing is crowd-pleasing rubbish.'

Glenys shrugged. 'It isn't all about the choice of music.'

'Before you go!' Jen was grinning like the Cheshire Cat. 'Well done everyone! We're through to Danbrook Spa!' She allowed them a minute of noise. 'But now it gets harder. Three new songs! In three weeks!' She didn't seem particularly daunted by the prospect. 'So I need everyone at rehearsals, on time and ready to sing. I've been working on an arrangement — see the confidence I have in you! — and I'll announce the songs on Wednesday. Solo parts, I'll contact you separately. Go and celebrate!' She made a shooing motion, and the choir began to leave, chairs scraping.

Pippa pulled out her phone and texted Simon. *We're through to the next round! All done, home in half an hour x.* When she pocketed her phone, Jen was still standing there. She looked — not sad, exactly, but lost.

'Are you OK?'

Jen jumped. 'Ooh, didn't see you.' She tried to smile. 'I just wish Claire was here.'

'I'm sorry,' said Pippa. 'I heard you were — close.'

'Yes,' said Jen, quietly. 'We were.' She walked to her seat and picked up her music case. 'She wouldn't have missed this for anything. So, yeah, it's bittersweet.' She paused. 'Anyway. Thank you for coming. See you Wednesday?'

'Yes, see you Wednesday.' Jen's straight black back marched off, merging with the other people leaving the hall.

I ought to be heading home...

Pippa sat and thought until a caretaker cleared his throat at her, then hurried out into the street.

She ought to be happy. They'd won third prize, and Jeff's secret, embarrassing, potentially worrying hobby was actually pretty cool.

But she was puzzled. She made her way to the car park, feeling as if she was trying to grasp something just out of reach. It still eluded her when she parked the Mini outside Laurel Villa. Pippa resigned herself to whatever it was being driven from her head by nappies and dinosaurs and breadsticks, and plastered a smile on her face as she walked up the drive. Time to be Mummy again.

CHAPTER 18

'So, dear, what's this big secret that you want me to help with?'

It had seemed like such a good idea at the time. But now that Sheila was actually here, in her sitting-room, it was hard to know where to begin.

The minute hand of the clock was already creeping to the top again. Pippa set her mug on the coffee table and took a deep breath.

'It's about Claire,' she said.

'Claire?' Sheila looked completely taken aback. 'Oh, Claire.' Her expression took on a regretful, saintly air. 'Poor Claire.' Then she frowned. 'But — I didn't think you knew her.'

'That's the problem,' said Pippa. 'Promise not to tell anyone?'

Sheila nodded, shifting to the edge of her seat.

'Say "I promise",' Pippa prompted.

'Of course I promise. Don't be silly, dear.' Sheila waved a dismissive hand. 'Now come on — out with it!'

Pippa had to drag the words out of herself. 'I think there's something fishy about Claire's death.'

Sheila's eyes boggled. 'You mean — murder?'

'I'm not sure,' said Pippa. 'But it's an option.'

Sheila sipped her tea, considering. 'And how would I be helping, exactly?' She regarded Pippa with narrowed eyes.

'You know the family, for one thing. You're friends with Claire's mother. You were at the funeral, and the reception. You've lived here for ages, and know everyone, so you can get into conversations and ask questions I couldn't.'

'Oh!' breathed Sheila. 'So I'd be a sort of — undercover agent?'

'Erm, yes.' Pippa mentally drew a line through the word *assistant*. 'An associate.'

'So we'd be partners!' exclaimed Sheila. 'Partners in crime! I did love that series when it was on. The hats, and the dresses, and the cars…'

'I don't think you'll need any special outfits,' Pippa laughed. 'Just a good set of eyes and ears.'

Sheila smirked. 'Oh, I have those, don't you worry.'

'Excellent.' Pippa decided it was time to get professional. 'So, did you notice anything unusual at the reception?'

Sheila mused over her cup. 'Unusual… Not particularly. But then, no funeral is the same, is it?' She reached for a biscuit. 'I was surprised they only had a pub buffet. Not very suitable, in my view. But then again, they were taken by surprise. It wasn't expected.' She gazed into the distance. 'Or was it?'

'How did you think her husband seemed?'

'Pete? Well, he wasn't exactly devastated, was he? Unless he was hiding it. Stiff upper lip and all that, although men aren't meant to hold it in these days, are they? Letting it all hang out.' Sheila leaned forward. 'And there was a rumour about that.'

'Letting it all hang out?' Pippa faltered.

'Exactly. All that *working away*.' Sheila tapped the side of her nose, and Pippa wondered how many bad sitcoms Sheila had watched over the years.

'Working away doesn't mean he's playing away,' she said, trying not to let defensiveness creep into her voice. 'Simon works away sometimes, and he'd never —'

'That's different,' Sheila said flatly. 'He's younger, more . . . under the thumb, so to speak. Not that that's a bad thing.' She regarded Pippa appraisingly.

'Let's stay focused on Pete,' said Pippa, gripping her mug tightly. 'Do you have any proof?'

'There were definitely shenanigans.' Sheila's eyes gleamed. 'Janet used to come to bridge club quite downcast. She wasn't the sort to talk openly, but she did mutter that there were days when she thought divorce wasn't such a bad thing, whatever the church said.'

'And she definitely meant Claire?'

'Oh yes. If you mentioned Pete's name it was like a bad smell to Janet. Someone even hinted that one of the women had an abortion!' She sat back, triumphantly.

'So Claire was a Catholic?'

'Oh yes, very much so. I don't think Pete's anything.' Sheila leaned in. 'And that was another thing. She'd always longed for a big family, and it didn't happen. Ovaries. I mean, two children is perfectly normal, of course,' she said hastily.

'So . . . if Pete had wanted a divorce, she wouldn't have let him have one?'

'Noooo...' Sheila shook her head. 'And I doubt he'd be

able to afford to keep her and the kids and set up with a fancy woman.'

'Hmm.' Pippa remembered Pete standing in front of the church. There was something . . . slick about him. Not unsavoury, but — slippery? Then she remembered his eyes seeking someone in the congregation, and the young woman in heels who had scuttled from the church early. One of Pete's women? But could she imagine him slipping poison into his wife's tea, or taking her GTN spray? If anything, the set-up allowed him to play the field. 'Can you think of anyone else who might be a suspect?'

'Not off the top of my head.' Sheila bit a precise arc from her biscuit and replaced it in her saucer. 'She was a nice woman, but not outstanding in any way, if you know what I mean. Not wealthy, not a career woman, not a sex goddess. Just a perfectly normal woman living a normal life. Not the sort of person to get murdered at all.' She regarded Pippa thoughtfully. 'Are you sure you're on the right track?'

'If I was sure, I'd have got the police on board,' Pippa retorted. She sighed. 'Sorry, Sheila. It's just — you know when you have a hunch…'

'Woman's intuition,' Sheila said, sagely. Pippa tried not to make a face. 'I shall do what I can to help.'

It came to Pippa in a flash. 'I know what you could do.'

Sheila raised her head languidly. 'What, dear?'

'You could find out what medication Claire was taking. Pop round one evening, say you're going to the pharmacy tomorrow to pick up your prescription, and offer to drop off Claire's leftover tablets and stuff.'

'Ooh yes. And I bring them to you?'

'And you bring them to me.'

'I might even be able to get Pete to tell me about Claire's health!' exclaimed Sheila.

'Maybe not,' said Pippa hurriedly. 'Make the offer, and listen to what he says. He'll probably be glad of one less job to do.'

'I shall have to invent a plausible ailment for myself,' mused Sheila.

'Just cough a bit. Would you like another cup of tea?'

Pippa took the cups to the kitchen. As the kettle boiled she leaned her elbows on the worktop. Sheila wasn't exactly the partner she would have chosen. In fact, if she'd made a list Sheila would probably have been near the bottom. But to give her her due, it did look as if she would be useful. Providing Pippa could get her to keep things subtle.

'I've thought of something else,' said Sheila brightly, as Pippa took the tea through.

'Oh yes?' Pippa put the cups on the coffee table.

'Two things, in fact.' Sheila smoothed her skirt. 'The choir, and the charity shop Claire volunteered in. We need to cover all bases.'

'Mm.' How long would it take for Sheila to have a map with pins in it on her wall? 'The choir I know about, mostly. Any discontent there seems to be directed at Jen. There was some muttering in the altos — but Claire was a soprano.'

'But what if the — whatever it was — was aimed at Jen, and went wrong?' Sheila was bouncing in her seat.

'In that case Jen would need to have a heart complaint, and as far as I know, she doesn't.'

'Well, you'd better find out then.' Sheila said, crisply.

'I'll see what I can do. What about the charity shop?'

Sheila looked very wise. 'Not that I frequent charity shops, you understand, but on the rare occasions that I do venture in, the assistants always bicker. An item's overpriced, or they think the window display could be better. Perhaps someone there was angry with her over some small thing, and planned to teach her a lesson. *A lesson which went wrong,*' she intoned.

'I suppose it's possible,' said Pippa. 'I'll pop in.'

'Is there anything else I should know?' asked Sheila.

Pippa debated whether she should mention the Jen and Claire thing. 'I don't think so.' The thought of Sheila very deliberately not mentioning it in a conversation with Claire's family was too awful to contemplate.

'So our plan of action —' Sheila ticked the items off on her fingers. 'Me — visit Pete and obtain her leftover medication. You — visit the charity shop and pump the assistants for intel. When do we report back?'

'Erm, if we find something?'

'Excellent. I'll be in touch.' Sheila levered herself up from the sofa and shook hands with Pippa.

'Thanks. And Sheila — don't say anything to Simon, will you?'

Sheila snorted. 'Of course not.'

'Not even a hint.'

Sheila smiled indulgently. 'Not even a hint. I'll let myself out.'

At the sound of the front door closing the baby alarm crackled into life. 'Here we go,' said Pippa, running upstairs. To be fair, Ruby had slept for an hour, and was probably overdue for a feed. She was waving her fists in the air, but her cry was an *I want attention* cry, not an *I am furious* one. Within two minutes she was in Pippa's arms and feeding peacefully.

I ought to remember how lucky I am. I don't have to work, I have two lovely, mostly well-behaved children, and a husband who loves me. And I live in a pretty village.

If people wouldn't keep dying.

She shooed the thought from her.

If Sheila didn't manage to put her foot in it somehow, and give the game away to Simon.

What are the chances of —

Pippa bit her lip. She suddenly felt warm. But there was nothing to be done. Sheila had her orders — or had she given orders to her? — and she was part of this now, whether Pippa liked it or not.

Ruby finished off and looked at Pippa expectantly, a little dribble of milk running down her chin. Pippa swapped sides and Ruby set hungrily to work. Just enough time for her to finish before they needed to fetch Freddie. She reached for her phone and searched for the Gadcester Hospice Shop. Closed Monday afternoons. Typical. Oh well, there was always the rest of the week. She let Ruby's sucking lull her into a state of non-thought. If only she could feel that way more often.

CHAPTER 19

Pippa basked in smugness as she wheeled Ruby towards the church hall. Sheila had already begun to carry out her mission; Pippa had received a text yesterday evening. *Got them! Won't say more in case this is bugged but . . . coffee Wednesday?*

Pippa had replied *Yes please*, feeling rather inefficient.

But today was bright and sunny, she could visit the charity shop with the children later, and there was also the delightful prospect of no Sam at playgroup. No more backbiting, no more snarky comments. *And* she was early. She fished for her keys, and opened the door.

Ten minutes later she looked at her watch. The toys were out, it was five minutes to ten, and no-one here yet. How odd. It was Tuesday, wasn't it?

Imogen drifted in with Henry. 'Sorry I'm a bit late —' She broke off as she took in the emptiness of the room. 'Not just me, then.'

Caitlin and Eva arrived shortly afterwards, and Pippa heaved a sigh of relief. 'I was beginning to think something was wrong.'

'No,' said Caitlin, 'not really. Are you all right?'

'Yes, fine.' Pippa pushed her hair back. 'Bit hot from shifting toys, but otherwise —' She looked more closely at Caitlin. 'Why wouldn't I be?'

'Well, um,' Caitlin shifted uncomfortably from one foot to the other. 'You were a bit, er, poorly last week, weren't you.'

'That was because Sam was a bitch,' Pippa snapped. 'I'm fine now.'

'Good,' murmured Caitlin, and went to help Imogen with the chairs.

Slowly, more people trickled in. Some seemed just as normal, attending to their children, settling down with bags and toys. But some seemed to be avoiding her eye.

This is ridiculous.

Pippa cleared her throat. 'Excuse me.'

She said it so quietly that half the room hadn't noticed. 'Excuse me!'

This time the chatter stopped. 'Sorry to interrupt, but, um, what happened at the last session wasn't normal procedure. Sam's been having a go at me for a while, and it got to the point where I wasn't prepared to put up with it any longer. I have no intention of banning anyone else from the group. It was a one-off. If Sam apologises, I'll think about letting her back in.' Her cheeks were burning. 'Announcement over, carry on.' Most people resumed their conversations, but a few glances lingered on Pippa.

The door swung open and Bella ran in, followed by Lila. 'What time d'you call this?' grinned Pippa.

'I went to yours first,' said Lila. 'I think I just missed you.'

'Why? That's right out of your way.'

'Let me get Bella settled, and I'll come and chat.'

'Oh, OK.' Pippa went to a vacant chair near Caitlin, who stopped her chat and beamed brightly, then carried on talking. Something about nappies. *Whatever.* Pippa watched Lila put her bag down, rummage for a snack, find Bella a selection of toys. She seemed tense. And she wasn't usually this attentive to Bella. *What's up?*

Perhaps she knows about Jeff. Pippa had seen the photos from SingFest UK in the centrefold of yesterday's *Gadding Messenger*. Admittedly they had come out quite grainy, but the one of heat winners Short Back And Sides was bigger, and Jeff was right in the middle of the picture.

If you knew it was Jeff. He did look different without his suit and glasses, and with the addition of the quiff. How likely was Lila to a) buy the *Gadding Messenger*, b) see the SingFest photos, c) connect her shy boyfriend with the grinning biker lifting a trophy?

So what was it?

The door opened again, and Serendipity appeared with Monty on a lead. 'Do you have a minute, Pippa?' Her voice was normal, friendly, but she held herself stiffly and her smile was strained.

What's going on?

Pippa gazed around the room. Lila was getting up from the floor, with an unreadable expression on her face. Everyone else was not looking her way.

Emphatically so.

Pippa had always thought that when people said they felt a shiver down their spine, they were being melodramatic. Now she knew better. A feeling of utter dread came over her, and her stomach contracted. She wanted to get up and run from the room. Lila was coming. Whatever it was, whatever had happened, she could tell from Lila's face that she was about to find out.

'What's up?' she said, and the words seemed ridiculously flat and trivial.

Lila turned in the direction of the back rooms. Pippa got up and followed. She was in a dream, a piece on a chessboard, moving perhaps to her doom. Out of the corner of her eye she saw Serendipity hesitantly moving in their direction, but she could not stop. She could not stop.

Lila held the kitchen door open for her, then shut it behind them. 'Have you seen the paper?' she asked.

Pippa could have cried with relief. 'The *Messenger?* Yes, I knew they were taking photos at the competition —'

'Not the *Messenger*.' Lila pulled her phone from her pocket. 'The *Gadcester Chronicle*.'

'No, what's in the *Chronicle*?'

A light knock on the door made them both jump. Lila hurried to the door and peeped out. She stayed there for a moment, listening to the other person, then sighed and opened it to reveal Serendipity. 'She's seen it, too.'

'I'm sorry, Pippa,' said Serendipity, pulling a newspaper from her bag. 'I found it online.' She handed Pippa the newspaper. 'It's on page 5. The Opinion column. Sit, Monty.'

Pippa spread the paper out on the worktop. She felt Lila's arm at her waist, and pushed it away.

<u>Opinion</u>

WATCH YOUR BACK

by Janey Dixon

A few months ago I wrote about a very — busy — woman in Much Gadding.

Yesterday, I had the pleasure of acting as a judge in the Gadcester SingFest UK competition, and I was in the same room as she was.

I will stress that I didn't speak to her. I didn't even recognise her. But she was there.

Spying.

Being a busy person is one thing. Joining a choir for the purpose of snooping is another. Particularly when a member of that choir has recently died an unexpected but natural death. And yet nothing can be done. It is not illegal. Merely in exceptionally bad taste.

I will not dwell on the ghoulish behaviour of this person, as I feel it is unsuitable for a family newspaper. I will not name her, since her husband and children do not deserve to suffer. I will, however, say that the quicker she drops her sleuthing ambitions and returns to homemaking, the better for all concerned.

In the meantime, watch your back. Be careful what you say.

For all you know, *she* is there.

Taking notes.

The words danced before Pippa's eyes. Blood pulsed in her ears. Bile rose in her throat, and she ran to the sink, retching.

'I'm sorry,' said Serendipity. 'I thought you ought to know.'

'I'm going to kill Sam,' Pippa told the sink. 'I am, actually, going to kill her. How dare she set Janey Dixon on me?' Her voice rang out, amplified by the porcelain.

'How *dare* she?'

'I know,' said Lila. 'She's a Grade A bitch. But you already knew that. She's just gone up a level.'

'What can I do?' Sweat prickled on her scalp. She turned to Serendipity. 'You're a public person, you know about this stuff. What can I do?'

'I'm not sure,' said Serendipity, slowly. 'The thing is, she hasn't named you. Yes, someone who knows you could work out who you are —'

'And already has,' said Pippa, stabbing a finger in the direction of the main hall.

'I'm afraid so. But really, will you sue the paper? Are you going to take it through the courts?'

'No.' Pippa hung her head. 'I'd die of embarrassment. And Simon would kill me. I'm just glad he doesn't read the paper.' A horrible thought struck her. 'Oh God, what if someone at work tells him?'

'You'll know if they do,' said Lila.

'The thing is,' said Serendipity, very reasonably, 'even if you write a stiff letter to the paper, all they have to do is print a little sorry note at the bottom of page 59, and they're done. It probably isn't worth bothering.'

'I can't let her get away with this,' Pippa growled.

'I didn't say that,' grinned Serendipity. 'But I wanted to let you know so that you can deal with any flak.'

'She's a lot calmer than me,' said Lila. 'I'd give that cow a black eye.'

'So...' Serendipity paused. 'The urn won't be hot yet, will it?' She put a hand to the metal, then laughed at Pippa's surprised expression. 'To make a cup of tea. I wasn't planning to go after Sam with a mug of boiling water.'

Pippa snorted. 'I'd need something bigger than a mug.'

'You don't mean that,' said Serendipity.

Pippa considered. 'No. I s'pose not. What I will do, though, is tell the group that I've seen the article and it's a load of rubbish. Otherwise they'll tiptoe round avoiding me.' She was about to march out when Serendipity put a restraining hand on her arm.

'Maybe you should do that at your choir, too,' she murmured.

Pippa's mouth dropped open. 'I never thought of that! And —' she riffled through the paper, 'there are photos of SingFest in here, too!' She put her head in her hands. 'They'll rumble me for sure,' she muttered through her fingers.

'Remind them that you joined before what's-her-face died,' Lila said, soothingly.

'Yes, but — I won't be able to ask any questions, will I?' Pippa buried her head in her hands again. 'Just when we were getting somewhere,' she mumbled.

'Woah,' said Serendipity. 'Do you mean — you *are* snooping?'

Pippa lifted her head, expecting to see disgust on Serendipity's face. But she actually looked impressed. 'Um, I prefer "investigating". Or "making enquiries", that would also be good.'

'Whatever. You really think there might have been another murder?'

'It's hard to say,' Pippa declared, more confidently. 'There isn't much evidence. But something feels wrong.'

'Did you recruit your sidekick?' Lila grinned.

'Yes,' Pippa smiled back. 'She thinks she's my partner.'

'OK, this is turning into some sort of TV show,' said Serendipity. 'If you need anyone to knit the murderer into submission, or tie them up with bunting, I'm your woman.'

'I'll be in touch.' Pippa smoothed her hair. 'Do I look fairly normal?'

'As much as ever,' Lila assured her.

'Thanks for that. I'll go out and tell them.'

Monty barked. 'All right, Monty,' said Serendipity. 'Time for your walk.' She picked up his lead and he rose, shaking his mane like a shampoo advert.

Pippa held her head high as she stalked into the main room. 'I have an announcement to make.' She looked at her audience. Even the toddlers were watching. She'd better mind her language.

'Until now I hadn't seen the Opinion column of yesterday's *Gadcester Chronicle*. I gather that many of you have, and guessed that it's about me. I imagine that's why we're light on numbers today, too.

I joined the choir before the — passing — of Claire Staunton. I don't know why Sam — and it clearly is Sam — has chosen to attack me by passing lies to a local paper. However, I'm not going to do anything formal. I'd even be prepared to welcome Sam back to the group.' She took in their astonished expressions, and grinned. 'When hell freezes over.' That drew tentative smiles, and already the atmosphere seemed less overcast as she walked to her chair.

Caitlin, on her way to the kitchen, hesitated for a moment, and then approached. 'Good for you,' she said quietly. 'Sam's a poisonous cow, and the less you react, the better. She tried to get me on her side, but I told her to get knotted.' Her eyes fell to the newspaper, which Pippa had stuffed in her bag. 'So what's this SingFest thing?'

'It's a choir competition. The heats for the one they have on the telly. Our choir got through to the next round.' Pippa picked up the paper and riffled through it to the pictures. 'That's us. I'm in the second row — there.'

'Ooh yes, so you are,' said Caitlin. 'Is that Ritz Robertson in the pink suit? He cracks me up.'

'Yeah, that's him. See that frizzy-haired woman?' Pippa almost poked her finger through the page. 'That's Janey bloody Dixon.'

'The newspaper columnist?' Lila leaned over to inspect the photograph. 'She left her broomstick in the corner, then.'

'Mm.' Pippa paused, and a little spark of devilment made her carry on. 'We came third. This choir came second, and these were the winners.'

'Uh-huh.' Lila scanned the page without interest. 'Impressive motorbike.'

Pippa was tempted to make some sort of comment about a ride, but perhaps that would be taking things a little too far. Besides, she still wasn't sure how Lila would take it, or whether Jeff would come clean. She hoped he would. But for now, she'd concentrate on her own problems, thank you very much.

CHAPTER 20

'What we doing next, Mummy?' Freddie asked, abandoning his fish fingers.

'Going on a trip to Gadding Magna.' Pippa braced herself.

'What's there?'

'I'm not sure. We'll go and find out.'

'Is there a playground?'

'I don't know. Maybe.'

'Shops?'

'Yes, there are shops.'

'OK.' Freddie harpooned a piece of fish finger, while Ruby fed peacefully. 'But why?'

'Why not,' Pippa said, looking at Ruby's head and wishing she could silence her older child as effectively.

Once lunch was finished and all traces had been removed from the children, Pippa loaded the Mini with the essentials for a trip; pushchair, changing bag, snacks for Freddie, small toys for both children, and finally carried Ruby out in her car seat. Oh, for the days when going anywhere wasn't an expedition.

The road to Gadding Magna was wider than most of the

roads which led out of Much Gadding. It was probably the road that Pippa was least familiar with, though that would change when Freddie went to high school. She almost laughed out loud at the thought of it. As if Freddie would ever be old enough for high school. The Mini pootled past fields and a country pub, and eventually a house or two popped up. Then came side streets, a new housing estate, and finally a road sign festooned with hanging baskets — *Gadding Magna: twinned with Steinbaden. Best Kept Large Village 2005.*

Pippa eased the Mini into a small, half-empty car park on a side street. 'Here we are!' she said, brightly. In the rear view mirror, Freddie's mouth was turned firmly down. 'Let's go and explore.'

'Don't wanna,' grumbled Freddie.

'We don't have to stay too long,' Pippa wheedled. 'Mummy needs to do a couple of things.'

'What sort of things?'

Perhaps Freddie would become a detective, or possibly an interrogator, when he grew up. 'Just . . . things.' She unloaded Ruby and put the car seat onto its wheeled frame. At least one of them was powerless to resist.

Ruby smiled, and a smell floated up from her which made Pippa recoil.

'Ruby did a poo, Mummy!' shouted Freddie, backing away and pointing. 'Pooooohh!'

'Ssshh, Freddie!' Pippa looked for a public toilet, but there were none in sight. She sighed, opened the boot, and spread out the changing mat.

Ruby gurgled happily as Pippa wiped her. 'I'm glad you're pleased,' said Pippa, sliding the toxic nappy into a plastic bag. 'I'm certainly not.' Then again, she consoled herself, at least Ruby hadn't done it while she was in the charity shop. That would definitely have impeded her investigations.

The charity shop was on the main street, as, Pippa suspected, were most things in Gadding Magna, which despite its name, was not much bigger than Much Gadding. She stopped to survey the scene. The village — or large village, to be completely accurate — looked as if it had had a makeover in the seventies, adding a concrete parade of shops. Opposite, a sign pointed down a smaller road: *Gadding Magna High School.*

'Let's go and see the big school, Freddie.' She didn't want to go into the charity shop yet. *Am I scared of what I'll find? Or scared I'll find nothing?*

Freddie gripped her hand tighter and tighter as the tall blocks loomed ahead. 'We're not going in, are we?'

'Noooo,' said Pippa. She wondered where Jen would be, which building she taught in. 'Daddy went to this school, you know.'

'Don't be silly, Mummy!' Freddie giggled. 'Daddy's too old for school!'

'He was a little boy once, you know. And I was a little girl.'

'No you weren't,' said Freddie, with an air of finality. He tugged her hand. 'Can we stop looking at it now?'

They walked back to the main road, and Pippa noted that it would take no more than two or three minutes to get from the school gate to the parade of shops. There was a newsagent's next to the charity shop, which probably did a roaring trade in sweets and ice lollies, and on the other side was a small wine bar, whose sign said *Luigi's* in shiny silver script. Was that where the teachers went for a

Friday-afternoon drink? Or did they go to — she peered up the street — the Lamb and Flag?

The charity shop itself was pretty unremarkable. A purple plastic sign, *Gadcester Hospice Shop*, and a window display of three headless mannequins in jumpers and skirts; one red, one cream, one grey. A poster on the door showed a smiling woman gazing across a counter while handling a scarf: *Care To Volunteer? Volunteer To Care*. Of course; they had lost a helper. Pippa's smile faded, and she pushed open the door.

The shop was small and cluttered. Rails of clothes lined the walls, arranged by type and colour, and further revolving stands held blouses, skirts, jumpers and bags. Every time Pippa moved she feared she would knock something down.

'Can I help you?' A fiftyish woman in an outfit rather like the ones in the window leaned over the counter.

'I'm just browsing,' said Pippa, steering Ruby on a slalom course towards the bookshelves.

'Toys! Yeah!' Freddie ran to the small display of plastic and metal whatnots and rummaged in a basket full of cars.

Pippa scanned the bookshelves, but as she read she became aware that she was being watched. She turned and the assistant was hovering behind a small cabinet of costume jewellery nearby.

Pippa turned to face her. 'Did you want to ask me something?' she said, as pleasantly as she could.

The assistant began to rearrange a few strings of beads on a revolving stand. 'We're short-staffed,' she remarked to the stand.

'Oh, I'm sorry,' said Pippa. She pulled a book out and read the blurb.

'It isn't easy being in the shop on my own, you know.' The woman sounded defensive. 'And we have a lot of schoolchildren in, who need monitoring.' She peered at Freddie, who was running a toy car along the carpet join.

Pippa slid the book back into place. 'I'm sure they do. The shop must be busy at lunch and after school.'

'Yes. You've caught us at a quiet time.' The assistant allowed herself a brief, tight smile, which was gone as quickly as it came.

'I saw the poster on the door. About volunteers.'

The assistant brightened immediately. 'Would you be interested?'

'Um, not right now.' Pippa pointed at the two children. 'Have some of your volunteers left, then?'

'We've lost a couple, yes,' said the assistant, fingering a stack of espresso cups.

'I think I knew someone who used to work here.' Pippa moved closer. 'A lady named Claire.'

The assistant immediately assumed a sorrowful expression. 'Oh yes, Claire. That was terrible. I read it in the paper and I couldn't believe it. I mean, she didn't seem ill at all.'

'No. And I suppose you'd have seen her a lot, in the shop.'

'Well yes, until recently. But Claire left us in early January.'

'Oh!' Pippa tried not to appear pleased at this information. 'I didn't know.'

'It isn't the sort of thing one talks about.' The assistant looked round the otherwise empty shop, and lowered her voice. 'The thing is, there were problems in the shop. Money going missing.'

'Really?' Pippa glanced at Freddie, who was weighing up the merits of two toy cars. 'Gosh.'

'Yes. Not much, just ten or twenty pounds a week. The first time, Jill — the manager — thought it was someone borrowing from the till. The cashpoint is right at the other end of the street, you see, so someone might pop to the shops on their break. With every intention of putting the money back later, of course. When they'd been to the cashpoint.'

'Of course,' Pippa assured her, wondering how many times she had borrowed money.

'So Jill had a word with all of us, and a couple of people got quite heated.'

'Oh, and Claire was one of them?'

'Noooo,' said the assistant, leaning on the cabinet. 'She wasn't that sort of person. Very calm. Understanding, if you know what I mean. But she left shortly afterwards, with one of the people who *had* made a bit of a scene. And you know what?' She paused dramatically.

'No, what?' Pippa suspected she knew the punchline already, but she couldn't spoil the assistant's big moment.

'It stopped, right away. No more missing money!' The assistant pursed her lips. 'You can draw your own conclusions, I'm sure.'

'Mm,' said Pippa.

'Can I have both cars, Mummy?' asked Freddie, holding them up as high as he could. 'I can't choose.'

'We'll see,' said Pippa. 'How much are the toy cars, please?'

'Twenty pence each,' the assistant replied promptly.

'I think my budget will stretch that far.' Pippa went to the pushchair and found her purse, then followed the assistant to the till. A ring binder was open on the counter, displaying a staff rota. Pippa handed a pound to the assistant, and took in as much as she could from the page while her change was being put together. 'Thank you.' She put ten pence into a box on the counter, and turned. 'Oh, what size is the jumper in the window? The red one?'

'I'll go and look.' The assistant weaved her way between the racks to the window. Pippa unlocked her phone and snapped the staff rota, then flipped to the front of the binder. As she'd expected, a list of names and phone numbers was stuck inside the cover.

'It's a twelve,' called the assistant. 'Would you like to try it on?'

'Yes please,' said Pippa, and photographed the list before turning hurriedly to the original page. The assistant finished wrestling the jumper off the mannequin and bustled back.

'Here you are,' she said, breathlessly. 'It's an Edinburgh Woollen Mill one, you know. Quality.'

'Would you mind watching the children? I won't be a minute.'

'Of course. The changing room's in the corner. The green curtain.'

Pippa drew the curtain, ruffled her hair, and waited a decent amount of time, then emerged with a regretful expression on her face. 'Too small for me, I'm afraid.'

'Oh, I am sorry,' the assistant said, in much the same tone as she had used when discussing Claire's death. 'Would you like to try the grey one? I think that's a fourteen.'

'It was a red one I wanted,' lied Pippa. 'I'd better get on, anyway. The baby will need feeding soon, and I'm sure you have lots to do.'

'Oh yes,' the assistant said, taking the red jumper back to the window display. 'There's more to working in a charity shop than meets the eye, you know.'

'I'm sure there is,' Pippa agreed, as she shepherded Freddie out of the shop, clutching his new cars tightly. She steered him past the newsagent's, thankful that it didn't have a display of sweets or toys in the window.

'What now, Mummy?' Freddie looked up at her.

'Let's walk to the end of the street,' said Pippa. 'Keep your cars safe.'

She checked her watch. Half past two. The place would probably be over-run with kids in an hour.

'I can see green!' shouted Freddie, pointing.

'Yes.' She steered the pushchair carefully along. 'Maybe it's a park.'

It was a park, with a small playground. Freddie whooped and ran towards it, while Pippa found a bench and took out her phone. Ruby blinked at her. 'Don't even think about it,' Pippa told her. 'It's too cold to be doing that here.'

Freddie had climbed on a swing and was attempting to get himself moving, one toe stabbing at the ground. 'Push me, Mummy!' he wailed.

Pippa sighed and put her phone away. 'Coming, Freddie.' She wheeled Ruby next to the swings and gave Freddie a gentle push.

'Harder, Mummy. Wanna go upupup!'

Pippa reflected as she pushed, and waited, and pushed again, and waited, that there was probably a reason why detectives in books tended not to have children. How many mysteries would Miss Marple have solved if she'd had to keep stopping for nappy changes and juice breaks? And she mulled things over as the swing creaked on.

CHAPTER 21

Sheila hurried into Pippa's house as if she might be apprehended at any moment. 'I parked round the corner,' she said out of the side of her mouth. 'Hurry up and shut the door!'

'Yes, boss.' Pippa glanced at the empty street before closing the door.

'I'm in the sitting room,' called Sheila. 'Is Ruby napping?'

'Yes, she went down five minutes ago.' Pippa sat opposite. 'So, um, what have you got for me?'

'*Drugs*,' murmured Sheila, her eyes gleaming. She reached into her handbag, brought out a handful of small cardboard boxes, and laid them on the coffee table. 'Pete was ever so grateful. He said he'd never have thought of it.'

'Hmm.' *If Pete's OK with the idea, that suggests he hasn't meddled with any of it.* Pippa shifted forward in her seat and examined the boxes.

'I can tell you what's there,' Sheila said, smugly. 'There's Ramipril, which is used to treat high blood pressure. It's an ACE inhibitor. Whatever that is.'

'OK.' Pippa reached for the box and studied the pharmacy label. The date on it was January 18. 'So these are recent.'

'They all are.'

Pippa opened the box and drew out a few sheets of silver tablet casing. Most were intact. 'That fits. What else is there?'

'Atorvastatin. That's for high cholesterol, and the packs are mostly full. Same date. This is the one I'm interested in.' Sheila held up a small spray bottle, no bigger than a handbag-sized perfume bottle.

'The short name is GTN spray. It's to relieve angina symptoms.' Sheila passed the bottle over. 'Try it.' Her voice was eager, strained.

Pippa took the lid off the slim little spray. 'Do I need to shake it?'

'I don't know,' Sheila snapped. 'Just spray it.'

Pippa pressed her finger down. Nothing.

She shook the spray, and tried again.

Her eyes met Sheila's. 'It's empty.'

'Exactly,' said Sheila, grimly.

'Oh my God.' Pippa stared at the bottle. 'Someone's got hold of this, and emptied it.' She put the spray on the table as if it would burn her. 'I assume they wiped the spray, but still — fingerprints.'

'It doesn't bear thinking about,' said Sheila, shifting in her chair. 'That poor woman, feeling an attack coming on, and reaching for her spray — ohh.' She wriggled.

'Well, it looks as if you've found the murder weapon,' said Pippa. 'Now we need the motive, and the murderer. That's the tricky bit. I'm guessing this spray is the sort of thing you have with you all the time, like an asthma inhaler. So it was probably in Claire's handbag. All someone would need was access to that.'

It was Sheila's turn to ponder. 'When would she leave her bag unattended? And who would know that she had the spray in there?'

Pippa considered. 'She would have had the bag lying about at home. Someone could have got to it there. Or choir practice — but no, all the bags go at the side of the room. Someone would notice.'

'Maybe not, if they had a similar bag, or if they acted casual,' said Sheila.

'They'd have to take the spray somewhere, though. You couldn't do it in the room. Even in the bathroom, someone might hear. Unless —'

'Unless what?' Sheila leaned forward.

'Unless they went outside for a cigarette.' Pippa got up and fetched her notepad. 'I'll make a list of people who smoke at choir practice,' she said, scribbling.

'It could still have been Pete,' Sheila said, quite resentfully. 'He's got the most opportunity out of anyone.'

'I suppose...' Pippa paused, pen hovering. 'But then if he isn't at home much, perhaps not. And what's his motive? Claire's the reason he can play the field, if the rumours are true. Why would he change that?'

Sheila sighed. 'This detective thing is more complicated than I thought.'

'Charity shop!' exclaimed Pippa, stabbing at the page with her pen. 'The bag would probably sit in the back room, and whoever else was in would be able to get at it. The volunteers would have to stagger their breaks and lunches, so the other person could easily be alone with the bag. We don't know when that spray was emptied.' She reached for her phone. 'I went to the charity shop yesterday and got a picture of the staff rota.' She moved to sit beside Sheila. 'The manager's part-time, and usually there are two people in the shop.' She indicated with her finger. 'You can see who Claire was on duty with. Four different people, and any of them could have done it. Then she's Tipp-Exed out, along with someone else. This isn't the most important thing, though.'

'No,' Sheila agreed. 'But what is?'

'I'm probably reasoning backwards . . . but it must have been someone who knew Claire fairly well, and who meant to do it. It's not a random thing like putting poison in a cup on a tray. They would have had to know Claire well enough to know that she had a heart problem, and used a GTN spray. But I don't understand *why*.' Pippa rubbed at her frown. 'Everyone seemed to like her. She was inoffensive. Which is a horrible thing to say about someone, but you know what I mean?'

'Yes,' said Sheila. 'Not the sort of person who gets murdered.'

'But she did.' Pippa frowned. 'There's something else, too. Have you seen the *Chronicle* this week?'

'Why?'

Pippa sighed. 'I'll put the kettle on.'

Sheila followed her into the kitchen, and as the kettle seethed she told the story of Janey Dixon's newspaper article. 'Anyone at the choir will know she means me. Anyone interested in the murder will know that someone who has recently joined the choir is digging for clues. A simple search through previous columns would bring up my name. If we're saying the person who killed Claire meant to do it…'

'Then you'd better watch your back,' Sheila finished.

Pippa shivered. 'You know what? I'm going to phone PC Horsley. This —' she pointed dramatically to the GTN spray, 'this is evidence. Firmer evidence than we've had up to now.'

'What about the charity shop thing?' Sheila asked. 'You said that two people left, and there was — pilfering — going on. You could even argue that Claire had had her hand in the till, and the guilt became too much for her. She emptied the spray herself. It would be a matter of time till she *met her end.*'

'Urrgh.' Pippa considered. 'But she was a Catholic. That would be a form of suicide, wouldn't it? I'm pretty sure they don't like that sort of thing. If she wouldn't divorce Pete because of her religion, she definitely wouldn't commit suicide. Anyway, she didn't need money. She didn't have to work, and she'd volunteered there for years.' She pushed her fringe back. 'Why would anyone who volunteered at a charity shop steal from the till?'

'Sudden money troubles?' Sheila flicked the kettle on again. 'What will you do about choir, Pippa? Will you go — is it tomorrow?'

'It is.' Pippa swallowed. Her mouth was suddenly very dry. 'I'm not sure what sort of reception I'll get. And, as you said, I'd better watch my back. Some of the altos are grumpy at the best of times.'

'I know!' Sheila exclaimed. 'I'll come with you.'

'You what?' Pippa stared at her, a moment broken by the *ping* of the kettle.

'I'll come with you.' Sheila shrugged. 'A week away from bridge won't kill me.'

Pippa was surprised to find herself hugging Sheila. As

far as she could remember, it had never happened before.

'Just make the tea, dear,' Sheila mumbled into her shoulder.

As Pippa might have predicted, the baby monitor whinged into life as she raised the mug to her lips. 'Oh, Ruby.' She put the mug down and ran upstairs, returning a few minutes later with a smiling Ruby.

'Can I have a go?' Sheila reached for the baby. 'It's a very long time since I've seen you, Ruby-woo.'

Ruby mewed with delight, and her little legs kicked as Pippa passed her over.

'Should your mummy go to the police,' Sheila asked Ruby, bouncing her on her knee. 'Should she? Should she?'

Pippa felt as if a well-meaning parrot had taken possession of her mother-in-law. 'This is getting big. Big and — uncomfortable.' She gulped a mouthful of cooling tea. 'If the police pick it up, they'll be able to ask questions that I couldn't. They can pull people in and make them talk.'

'To an extent,' said Sheila.

Pippa checked her watch. 'I could go now. If they're open.' She picked up her phone and scrolled for *Police*. The number was still saved in her phone. She had considered deleting it, but never had. Just in case.

Two rings. Three. Pippa willed PC Horsley to pick up.

Click. 'You are through to Much Gadding police station. Unfortunately —'

Pippa thumbed the *End Call* button. *How dare Jim Horsley be out solving other crimes when I need help?*

'He'll probably be in later,' Sheila soothed.

'Later won't do! I'll have Freddie then!'

Sheila waved a dismissive hand. 'He probably won't even understand what you're saying.'

'He's a sponge. If he's not meant to hear it, he'll hear it. And he doesn't have to understand it to repeat it.' *Sheila isn't the only parrot in my life*, thought Pippa.

'Well,' Sheila kissed Ruby and passed her carefully to Pippa. 'If I'm accompanying you to choir tonight then I'll head off. Things to do. When will you pick me up?'

'Quarter to seven?'

Sheila nodded. 'I take it you're going to put those away,' she said, looking pointedly at the tablet boxes lying on the table.

'Oh gosh, yes.' Pippa put Ruby into her bouncy chair and swept the boxes into a plastic bag, which she shoved into her changing bag. 'They'll be safe there. It's not as if Simon'll be rooting in my changing bag any time soon.'

'Mm,' said Sheila, faint distaste on her face. 'I'll leave you to it, then. If anything comes up, message me.'

Once she had seen Sheila out, Pippa sat down and flicked through the pages of her notepad. It wasn't exactly a thrilling read. Scraps of sentences, the occasional underlined word, and far too many question marks. PC Horsley would probably have been reprimanded for such shoddy record-keeping.

But PC Horsley isn't on the case, and I am.

Pippa pushed her hair back.

On the case of a victim she didn't know, with everything against her, including, for God's sake, the local media, and her only useful ally was her mother-in-law.

She wasn't sure whether to laugh or cry.

CHAPTER 22

Stopping the Mini outside Sheila's compact semi, Pippa jumped as the front door was flung open and a raincoated figure, collar turned up, slammed the door and scuttled towards her. 'Step on it!' she hissed, flinging herself into the car and sliding down until only the top of her head showed above the window.

'Seatbelt first,' said Pippa. 'And Sheila —'

'What?' Sheila's head turned, and she had to pull her coat collar down to see at all.

'You're my mother-in-law. It's normal for me to pick you up in my car in the early evening. Anyone would think we were going to burgle someone's house.'

Sheila got herself upright with a great deal of huffing, and thrust her seat-belt into its holder. 'Did Simon say anything?'

'Not particularly.' Pippa moved off slowly. 'I don't think he's seen the newspaper article, and presumably no-one he works with has figured it out. Or if they have, they're keeping quiet.'

'Good.' Sheila mimed zipping her mouth shut. 'You haven't left any of the — gear at home, have you?'

'Sheila. For the last time —' Pippa indicated right. 'The drugs are in my changing bag, and my casebook is in my music folder.' Not that anyone would be able to decipher the scrawled speculations of an amateur sleuth among the reminders of dentist's appointments, measurements for curtains and birthday present lists that littered the pages of her notebook.

'I suppose it is all right for me to just turn up,' Sheila said, as they stopped at a zebra crossing for a pair of teenagers with a large dog.

'Yes, of course,' said Pippa. 'That's what I did. You don't even have to sing, if you'd rather not.' *Please don't sing*, she willed silently. She didn't want poor Jen to have a nervous breakdown at the new and discordant addition to her choir.

'Oh, I think I better had,' said Sheila airily. 'I mean, that's what we're there to do.'

'Yes,' said Pippa. 'We're starting new pieces tonight, so I expect we'll all be learning.' Hopefully Sheila would be put next to someone extremely loud, and would either follow their lead or be inaudible. 'What part do you sing? Soprano or alto?'

'It's been a while,' said Sheila, and looked out of the window for the remainder of the journey.

They arrived early at the church hall, and secured a spot by the entrance. A few other cars were there already. Some people were on the point of going in, while some sat in their cars, texting or listening to the radio.

'I'm not sure I can do this,' Pippa said. She felt a bit wobbly.

'Yes you can,' said Sheila sternly. 'If it gets really bad, you can always walk out.'

'Thanks for that. Come on.' Pippa left the car and waited for Sheila. Facing up to the choir was not as bad as being trapped in a confined space with Sheila in her current mood.

Pippa pushed the door open, and the conversation stopped.

She hesitated, and Sheila shoved her forward.

Pippa had never had to do a walk of shame before. Not of that kind, at any rate. She flung her head up and walked towards the small knot of people gathered at the far end of the room. Jen was among them, and the expression on her face was — not quite disgust, not quite anger. 'I'm surprised you're here,' was all she said.

'You've seen the article, then.'

'Someone sent it to me. Everyone's seen it.'

'You know that I joined the choir before — it happened.' Pippa kept as still as she could, though she was quivering inside.

'Yes.' Jen's eyes were fixed on her. But then it was as if a shutter came down. 'We have a competition to prepare for, and three new songs to learn. We don't have time to waste on gossip and rubbish, and we can't afford to lose any more people.' Her voice cracked on the last words, and she looked down for a moment, gathering herself. 'But if I hear any more rumours, or see *anything* —' Her eyes blazed. 'Do I make myself clear?'

'Yes, Jen,' murmured Pippa obediently, though she would like to have punched her. *Someone has been murdered*, she told herself. *You need to play ball. Stay dumb, and shut up.* But Jen's words had stung, and she smarted at the reprimand.

'We have a new person.' Jen's expression changed to

neutral. 'Hello.'

'I saw the SingFest UK photos of the choir in the *Gadding Messenger*.' Sheila beamed as if the previous conversation hadn't happened. 'I'm interested in joining.'

'Mm.' Jen did not look particularly enthusiastic. 'Well, we're learning three new songs and we have the regional competition in a fortnight, so I'm afraid you'll have to pick it up as we go. Can you read music?'

Sheila's confident smile vanished. 'Um…'

'You'll pick up the tune when you've heard it a few times. Soprano or alto?'

Sheila considered.

'Do you sing high or low?' Jen's speech was becoming a little more abrupt.

'I'm sort of in the middle,' Sheila said apologetically.

'I'll put you with the altos, then. Places, everyone, and let's get started.' As the group rearranged themselves, the door creaked open and a few more people drifted in, including Glenys and Siobhan. Glenys scuttled to her place, while Siobhan loped towards the altos. As soon as Jen saw her, her hackles seemed to rise. 'And where were you on Sunday, Siobhan?'

Siobhan turned to face her. 'I had food poisoning. Couldn't keep anything down for three days.' Her tone dared Jen to challenge her.

'OK. Fine. Next time, get someone to let me know.'

Siobhan made her way to the back of the choir. 'I won't be expecting a get-well-soon card, then.' Pippa kept her eyes firmly on the back of Edie's head. Edie, who had looked away when Pippa passed her.

Jen clapped her hands. 'We'll warm up in a minute, and then get cracking on the new pieces. But I want to make

175

one thing clear first. I expect you to be here on time and make maximum effort till we step off the stage at the regional heats. Yes, Short Back And Sides were amazing. Yes, there will be other choirs as good or better. But that doesn't mean that we turn up and do a half-arsed job. I've pulled a few all-nighters working on the new arrangements, and I expect you to pull your weight. So no dodgy hamburgers.' Her eyes looked past Pippa. 'No random electricians.' Her eyes flicked to Eileen, trying to hide behind someone else. 'No — *snooping*.' Pippa studied the floor until she was reasonably sure that Jen had finished casting the death ray. 'Let's get to work.'

'Is she always like this?' Sheila whispered.

'Sssh,' hissed Pippa. 'I'm in bother already.'

Jen headed for a large pile of paper stacked on a plastic chair. She separated out a stack of sheets, and passed them to the nearest soprano. 'As we did well with contemporary music, I'm keeping it in the mix. Anyone acquainted with Simon and Garfunkel?'

Most hands went up.

'Good.' Jen handed a pile of music to the tenors. 'John Dowland?'

Fewer hands went up, belonging to a different subset of the choir.

'Right.' Jen reached the basses. 'Carly Rae Jepsen? Ah, Simon and Garfunkel win the popular vote then.' Jen gave the remaining sheets to the altos, and grinned. 'Soloists, step forward.' Daphne and Edie advanced, and Gerry and Archie joined them.

'Here we go again,' someone muttered behind Pippa.

Jen's grin vanished. 'Who said that?'

Silence.

'What did I say about gossip and rubbish?'

Still silence. A few people shuffled their feet.

'Do you think, with everything that has happened, I have time to organise some sort of Gadding's Got Talent to find a new set of soloists?' Jen glared at everyone in turn. 'Here's the deal. If you don't like the way I run things, you can either shut up or get out.'

'Then I'm out.' Siobhan pushed her way to the front. 'I don't like your music, or your attitude. In fact, Jen, I don't like you.' She came right up to Jen, and Pippa noticed that she was a good half a head taller. 'I've seen enough of you to last me a lifetime.' She stepped back, her lip curling. 'Good luck with whatever pile of crap she's given you this time, folks.' She strolled to the door, and as Jen turned to the choir, Siobhan gave her the finger. The door closed on a volley of shocked exclamations.

Jen shrugged. 'A bad apple gone.' She took her baton from the music stand and cleared her throat. 'Our soloists have had their parts for a few days, and I've asked them to practise, though of course they haven't done it together yet. Most of their parts are the same as yours, so this gives you the flavour of it.' She raised her baton. 'Welcome to the world premiere of our set for the regional heats.' She nodded to the four people stood in front of her, and her baton flicked *one-two-three-four*.

Pippa desperately tried to follow Edie's part on the photocopied sheets. It was amazing, but so intricate that she despaired of learning it in two weeks. Some people seemed relaxed; but others' bewildered expressions indicated they were thinking much the same as she was. And then Edie sang 'Flow, my tears,' and it was all Pippa could do not to cry.

The quartet transitioned effortlessly from the Dowland into 'Bridge Over Troubled Water'. Jen's eyes shone, and the corners of her mouth lifted. By the end, as the audience broke into clapping, she was grinning and wiping her eyes.

'It'll do, then?' She leaned on the music stand, looking as if she had just run a race. And in a way, Pippa thought, she had.

'Let's get to work.' Jen's raised voice cut through the excited, rising buzz in the choir. 'We're very short of time, so I propose we split into our sections. Your soloist and transition leader will take you through the part until break. Then we'll get together and try it as a whole.'

The soloists beckoned their sections into the four corners of the room. Edie, despite (or was it because of?) her Moomin sweatshirt, was brisk and businesslike. 'Ignore what they're doing,' she said, jerking her head at the cacophony behind them. 'Let's go up to the first transition. I'll give you the note.'

Sheila nudged her. 'She doesn't mess around, does she?' Her tone was half-laughing, half-impressed.

'No,' Pippa whispered back. 'She doesn't.'

They were so busy working through the different pieces and the transitions that break came out of nowhere. But when Pippa checked her watch it really was eight-thirty. Then again, she felt drained. 'Come on, let's get a brew,' she said to Sheila. 'How are you finding it?'

'Scary.' Sheila leaned close and muttered, 'I'm glad I'm only here as your minder.'

'But are you enjoying it?'

'I'm not sure enjoy is quite the right word.' Sheila grimaced. 'I'm enduring it.'

'Sorry.' They joined the fast-moving queue. Everyone

seemed to be in the mood to get on tonight. Conversation was limited. Pippa tried not to think about how no-one had spoken to her that evening, apart from Jen and Sheila. No one had even said hello. She served herself and Sheila, and took their cups to a pair of vacant chairs on the edge of a group.

'They're not very friendly, are they?' Sheila whispered, into the ear furthest from the group.

'I think you're condemned by association,' Pippa muttered. 'Hopefully they'll come round.' Mostly, sections were staying together. Glenys was chatting to Eileen and Daphne. The basses were laughing in the corner. Edie, at the far side of her own group, was clicking a sweetener into her drink. The woman next to her — was it Alison? — spoke. Edie smiled and dispensed a sweetener into her cup, and the woman stirred her drink thoughtfully with a plastic spoon.

'Drink up, everyone,' called Jen. 'Short break tonight. As you now know, we have a lot to do.' There was some grumbling, but it was good-humoured, and people rose willingly from their chairs. 'We'll try a run-through. I fully expect it to be a shambles, but we'll have a go anyway.'

The choir started together in fine style, but the wheels began to come off part-way through the first transition. 'Keep going!' Jen shouted, grinning. The altos and the sopranos were a whole beat apart. Daphne was making slow-down gestures to the sopranos. Someone giggled. 'Sopranos!' shouted Jen, waving. 'I'm over here!' The Dowland section, slow and sad, brought the choir back together, and the second transition was much better. 'We're getting there!' grinned Jen, her baton bouncing like a row of lambs jumping a fence.

The basses answered the altos.

The sopranos answered the tenors.

Everyone was smiling. And they all, somehow, finished together.

Jen put down her baton and applauded. 'For a first go, that was bloody brilliant,' she said. 'I'm so happy.' She blinked. 'Got something in my eye...' She rubbed it, and smiled. 'All right. Let's work on that first transition.'

It seemed no time until Jen said 'Let's call it a night.' She laid her baton on the stand. 'I'm very pleased with how tonight's session has gone.' Her gaze swept over the choir. 'See you next week. In the meantime, *learn your part*, and practise it as much as you can.'

The choir broke up into twos and threes, ambling to get coats, pick up bags, fish out keys. 'Come on, let's go,' Pippa said to Sheila, who seemed dazed. She handed Sheila her coat, shrugged into her own, and gathered up their belongings.

A slice of cold air hit Pippa as she opened the door. She huddled into her coat, holding the collar closed as she waited for Sheila.

'You took your time.'

Pippa stifled an exclamation. A smallish, roundish figure was standing next to her, out of the light. She blinked, trying to adjust her eyes to the darkness.

'We've met.' A woman's voice, and yes, she had heard it before. Pippa frowned, and looked again.

It was Carolyn.

CHAPTER 23

'If you've come to shout at me, please don't bother.' Pippa walked to the Mini and unlocked it.

'No. Wait.' Carolyn followed her.

'Pippa?' Sheila called from the door. 'Sorry, I was getting my coat on.'

'Over here,' called Pippa. 'What is it?'

'I have something for you.' Carolyn drew a small book from her pocket and handed it to Pippa. 'Claire's journal. She's written it ever since she was a teenager. I'm the only one who knows about it. Till now.' She sighed, looking at the ground, then faced Pippa. 'This is all that's left. Claire shredded each one when she finished it. She asked me, if she died, to get her journal and destroy it.'

'But — why me?'

'I read that piece in the *Gadcester Chronicle*,' Carolyn said, simply. 'I didn't know who you were at the funeral. I thought you were just another choir member. But when I saw what Janey Dixon wrote I decided to track you down.' Carolyn spread her hands. 'I need your help. I don't think Claire's death was natural, either.'

Sheila had caught up to them. 'Hello, Carolyn,' she

said, a little warily.

'Hello, Sheila,' Carolyn smiled. 'I assume you're in on this.'

Sheila drew herself up. 'I have no idea what you mean,' she said, nose in the air.

'Mum mentioned you offered to drop Claire's pills at the chemist,' said Carolyn. 'I take it Pippa's seen them.'

'Ah,' said Sheila. 'Um, yes.'

'I must go before anyone sees me,' Carolyn muttered. 'Mum has my number.' She hurried away, keeping out of the lights, and within seconds her small round shape was barely visible against the hedge. Then she was gone.

'Oh my gosh.' Pippa gazed at the space where Carolyn had been.

'Let's get into the car then,' said Sheila, a little peevishly. 'My feet are turning to ice.'

'Sorry.' Pippa opened the passenger door, then got in herself. The interior lights revealed the book as a slim exercise book with a thin floral cover. The pink square in the centre simply said *Notes*. Pippa opened the book and glimpsed neat, rounded writing. The book was a quarter full. 'I want to read it, but — we'd better get home. We're already late.'

'I suppose,' Sheila said regretfully.

Pippa started the engine and put her lights on. People were drifting out of the church hall. It was spitting with rain, and frost twinkled on the narrow grass verge. *Wonderful.* She turned the heater up and glanced at Sheila, who had the notebook in her lap. 'No sneaky reading, now.'

Once the way was clear, Pippa backed out. The Mini felt as if it was sliding. 'I'm taking my time, Sheila. I think the road's icy.'

'Oh dear.' Sheila gripped her seatbelt.

Pippa drove carefully forward, increasing her speed gradually. Another car shot past. 'Maniac,' muttered Pippa. But — no. It wasn't ice. The car seemed to be wobbling. Pippa looked for a place to pull over. But there wasn't anywhere. They were already out of Lower Gadding, and the unlit road stretched ahead. No bus stops. No side roads. 'It's no good,' she said. 'I'll have to stop on the road.' She steered as close to the edge as she could, fighting the car all the way, and let the Mini roll to a halt.

'What do you think it is?' Sheila quavered.

Pippa put the hazard lights on. 'Flat tyre, probably. It was fine when we drove here.' She checked carefully behind her before getting out.

It didn't take long to find the cause. A large, sharp nail was embedded deep in the wall of the driver's side front tyre.

Another car flashed by, and Pippa bit her lip. She had a spare tyre underneath the car, and a small toolbox in the boot. But there was no way she was going to change the wheel in pitch darkness, with cars zooming inches away. She got back into the car. 'I'm phoning the breakdown service. Keep your seatbelt on.'

The telephone operator assured her that someone would be there as quickly as possible. 'Given the circumstances you're a priority case, Mrs Parker. Try not to worry.'

'Thank you,' said Pippa. She pressed *End Call* and put her face in her hands.

'Don't worry, dear.' Sheila patted her arm. 'Anyone can get a flat tyre.'

'Not like this!' cried Pippa, tears streaming down her

face. 'The car was fine on the way out! Someone's stuck a nail in my tyre!'

'Oh,' said Sheila. When Pippa looked up she was staring straight ahead. 'The — the *swines*!'

'I'd better ring Simon.' Pippa wiped her eyes and blew her nose before dialling. *No sense in alarming him, too.*

He picked the phone up on the ninth ring. 'Hello?' He sounded wary.

'Simon, it's me. I've got a flat tyre. I've called the breakdown people. Hoping it won't take too long.'

'Oh, OK.' He swallowed whatever he was eating. 'Can't you change it?'

'I'm on an unlit country road. I'm prepared to swallow my feminist principles and let a man come and rescue me.'

'Sure thing. I'll save you some pizza.'

'How were the kids?'

'Fine, mostly.' *Crunch.* 'When did Freddie go off beans?'

'Dunno. I'd better get off the phone in case the breakdown people ring.'

'OK. Love you.'

'Love you.' Pippa pressed *End Call.*

Sheila shifted uncomfortably in her seat. 'How long do you think they'll be?'

'Not long.'

'It's very quiet out here, isn't it?' Sheila pulled her coat closer around her.

'Shall I put the radio on?'

Sheila nodded, and Pippa pushed the button.

'...and tonight on *SmoothTalk* we'll be discussing the safety of women in public places. Do phone in with your comments, the number is —'

She killed the radio, and her eyes fell to the slim book in Sheila's lap. 'Shall we read it?'

Sheila looked down at the book. 'Do you think we should? It feels — unlucky. To read about someone we think was killed, when we're alone in a car in the middle of nowhere —'

'About to be rescued. Come on, it's something to do.' Pippa opened the book and they huddled over it together. 'Tell me when you've finished reading and I'll turn the page.'

The journal began at January 1. A new book for a new year. Probably Claire had bought it for herself; it wasn't an elaborate, 'gift' kind of book. Each page was ruled in faint pink lines, with a little bunch of flowers at the top of the page. Claire's writing was easy to read, with large, rounded letters. Each i had a little circle instead of a dot, and her capital letters were a little bit fancy, with wavy tails and curls. 'I wonder what a graphologist would make of this,' said Pippa.

'I've read this page,' said Sheila. 'It isn't very exciting so far, is it? Just what they ate, and where she went, and how much she weighs.' She shrugged.

'Maybe it gets better.'

They read on.

January 4

P working away again tomorrow, this time he's off for two days. Took his grey suit to the dry cleaners in G Magna. Not sure why it needs cleaning.

The dry cleaners is a few doors down from the shop. Thought of popping in but — too soon.

'I assume she means the charity shop,' said Pippa.

Popped in to see J at the school before picking up suit. She showed me the new arrangements for SingFest, and played them on the piano. A sneak preview! She asked me to sing solo. I said I'd think about it. I probably will. She looked at me with such sad eyes. I wish she wouldn't. She makes me feel as if I'm letting her down. Perhaps I am.

January 6

Broke my New Year resolution to write every day less than a week in. But I can't write about yesterday. Too upsetting. Could feel my heart pounding and kept checking I had my spray, just in case. P safely off to London. C asked if I wanted her to pop round, but I'd already planned pizza and film night with the kids.

January 7

Eleven stone six pounds. I need to do something about this. But it's so hard to find time to exercise. I walk a lot, but it doesn't seem to make any difference. Went for a walk with C and we talked over choir. She isn't happy either. She's thinking of leaving, but I don't want to. It's the one thing I can enjoy without feeling guilty. Something pure. P back, seems to think it went well. Looks v pleased with himself. Smug. I wonder...

January 8

Family came for Sunday lunch. Mum fussing over my

health and what I had on my plate. Put a roast potato back and started crying, so ran upstairs.

I sometimes think —

January 11

Eleven stone four pounds. Mum rang to apologise. I know she only does it because she's worried, but I wish she wasn't so critical. And I don't want to know about so-and-so's daughter who lost all the baby weight in three months.

I HATE so-and-so's daughter!

January 12

Pete rang me from work, something's come up with a client and he has to go to Northampton to sort it out. Says he'll be back sometime tomorrow. Offered to take a bag in for him but he said he'd buy stuff at the station.

Am I being paranoid?

January 13

Eleven and a half stone. Maybe it's water retention. Talked to C about joining Weight Watchers or Slimming World but she says I'm fine as I am and it's just fads anyway.

January 20

Probably the worst week of my life so far. My hand's shaking even writing this. If it wasn't for J —

Sheila sighed. 'She leaves out all the good stuff.' She peered into the night. 'I thought we were meant to be a priority case.'

'There isn't much more to read,' said Pippa. 'We can probably finish it.'

January 22

Had a long talk with P and asked him to stop. He was so nasty. It makes me wish I could divorce him. I know I shouldn't think like that, but it's hard.
So much is hard.
And what about the children?
I couldn't live with myself.

January 24

I can't bring myself to write what I did.
What a hypocrite I am. After all the things I've said about P...

January 25

Thank God for C. She came round with a book mid-morning and I poured my heart out. She's such a good listener. She told me not to worry, and that everything would be fine. She even ran me a bath, and brought up a cup of tea and a magazine for me. I do feel better. Not so stressed. Looking forward to choir later.

The writing ended, and Pippa and Sheila's eyes met. 'I need to check the dates, but — I think that was Claire's last day.' Pippa closed the book.

'It isn't exactly helpful, is it?' Sheila said, with asperity. 'I'm not sure what Carolyn thinks we'll get from it. Most of the story's missing.' She sniffed. 'And names would be nice.'

'Mmm.' Pippa flicked through the book again. 'What I don't get is — why Carolyn gave me the book, instead of talking to me. She knows more than the book says; she must do!'

'Does she?' Sheila's brows knitted, then her face cleared. 'Ooh good, the recovery man's here.'

Pippa looked at the last page of the journal, at the rounded letters and the fancy capitals; the Ps, the Ts, the Cs, the Ss, the Gs, with their little tails and flourishes. She looked at the last page again — and she saw it. It was as if someone had taken away a filter, and the whole truth, the whole horrible truth, was staring her in the face. 'I *know*,' she said quietly.

'I was only saying,' Sheila said, somewhat aggrieved.

Pippa watched the big bright van back up. It stopped, and a man in overalls walked towards them, grinning.

'Yes,' she said. 'Let's get out of this mess.'

CHAPTER 24

'Are you sure this is a good idea?' Sheila asked, as she drove her neat little Peugeot into the car park.

'No,' said Pippa. 'Help me out, will you? Oh, and can you get Ruby's pushchair from the boot. I'll tell you how to unfold it.'

Sheila clicked her tongue. 'I have been a mother, you know. These things were far more difficult in my day.' She got out and shut her door sharply.

Pippa stood by as Sheila opened the pushchair and attempted to slot Ruby's car seat onto the frame. 'Remind me how this thing works again,' she said, eventually.

Pippa pointed with her free arm. 'Those bits slide into those bits.'

'Ohhh.' Sheila clicked the seat into place. 'Why don't they just put big arrows on it?'

'That would make it too easy,' said Pippa.

Sheila huffed. 'Hold your head up, for heavens' sake. You look as if it's going to fall off.'

Pippa ran a finger under her neck brace. 'This thing is so itchy.'

'It isn't for long,' Sheila said, stepping forward and

straightening it.

'Ow!' Pippa glared at her. 'It might be, if you do that again.'

'Come on.' Sheila locked the car and started walking, pushing Ruby in front of her. 'Let's go.'

The shop, as Pippa had expected, was quiet. Another customer, an elderly lady, was browsing the skirts, but hurried out when she saw Pippa, as if she were contagious.

Glenys was at the counter, sorting through a plastic bag of bead necklaces. A donation, presumably. She looked up at the squeak of the pushchair. 'Oh, um, hello.' Her eyes roved over Pippa, lingering on the neck collar and the sling. 'What happened?'

'I had a small car crash,' said Pippa. 'My tyre burst on the way back from choir and I drove into a hedge.'

'Oh. Gosh.' Glenys bustled out. 'Have you broken your arm?'

'No. It's a bad sprain, though.' Pippa's mouth twisted. 'At least it's my left hand.'

'Yes, yes,' Glenys said vaguely. 'Will you be able to sing?'

'I doubt it,' Pippa murmured. 'Everything hurts. I'm just glad it wasn't worse.' She unleashed the bravest smile she could. 'Anyway, I wondered if you could help. Have you got any button-through tops in a size fourteen? Sleeveless, if possible. Till I get this sling off.'

'I'll have a look,' said Glenys. 'Wait a moment while I get my colleague.' She walked to the back room and stuck her head in. 'Jill? I could do with some help. When you've got a moment.'

Seconds later a pleasant-faced woman with short blonde hair hurried through. 'Are these beads sorted yet?' she said.

'Mostly,' said Glenys. 'I'm chucking the ones to the right, they're too shabby to sell.' She scuttled to the racks, and studied them, her head on one side. She pulled out a few garments. 'How about these?'

'I'll try them,' said Pippa.

'The fitting room's here,' said Glenys. 'Do you need any help?'

'Sheila will give me a hand,' said Pippa. Sheila rolled her eyes, but remained quiet. 'If you wheel Ruby over, you can come in the fitting room with me.'

Sheila drew the curtain closed with an angry swish. 'How long are we keeping this up for?'

'Ssh,' said Pippa. 'Here.' She twitched a jungle-print blouse off its hanger. 'Give me a hand with this one.'

It took a fair bit of manoeuvring, but eventually the blouse was on. 'It really isn't your style, dear,' said Sheila.

'It fits, that's the main thing,' said Pippa. 'Let's try the one with the pink hearts on.'

The floorboards creaked. 'Everything all right?' called Glenys.

'Fine,' called Pippa. 'Not quite as easy as usual.' She looked at her reflection. The top did absolutely nothing for her. 'We've found two so far.'

'Jolly good,' said Glenys. The creaking moved away a little.

'Ugh,' Pippa whispered. 'Get me out of this before I throw up.' Once she was dressed, Sheila pulled the curtain back. 'I'll take these two,' Pippa called, walking to the till with Sheila and Ruby in her wake.

Glenys was at the counter, and her colleague had disappeared. 'Right,' she said, taking the hangers from Pippa. 'These two.' She took the hangers out and laid them on the desk, then read the tickets. 'That's five pounds twenty all together. Would you like a bag?'

'Yes, please.'

'That's another five pence then. Five pounds twenty five.' Glenys folded the blouses and put them into the bag. 'I hope you feel better soon.'

'Yes. Me too,' said Pippa. 'Hopefully this is the third bad thing.'

Glenys frowned. 'How do you mean?'

Pippa leaned against the counter, as if tired. 'Well, first Claire's unexpected death, obviously.'

'Obviously,' said Glenys.

'Then Siobhan got food poisoning, didn't she? And missed SingFest.' Pippa paused. 'Although maybe that was a good thing,' she said, softly. 'Siobhan's a bit of a rebel, and she doesn't like Jen. She might have chosen to cause trouble at the performance, and then Sweet Harmony wouldn't have got through to the next round. That would have been very disappointing.'

'Yes,' said Glenys. 'It would.' Her eyes flicked to the door.

'And then there's me,' said Pippa.

'Surely that's coincidence,' said Glenys, stepping back. 'Tyres can go at any time, if you don't get them checked.'

'But I do get mine checked,' said Pippa, standing up straight. 'And I don't usually find a big nail sticking out of my tyre.'

'You said it burst!' Glenys's eyes were wide-open now, and staring.

'My husband was furious when I told him what had happened. He insisted I rang the police. And they're checking the nail for fingerprints.'

Slowly, Glenys's shoulders relaxed. 'That's a good idea.'

'It is,' said Pippa. 'And you might get a phone call.'

Glenys froze, and stared at Pippa. 'Why?'

'The police want to interview everyone who was at choir on Wednesday. Just to check if they saw anyone hanging around. Kneeling by my car. That sort of thing.'

'The car park's very badly-lit,' Glenys said quickly. 'I doubt anyone saw much at all.'

'You were there before me on Wednesday, Glenys.' Pippa put her unbandaged hand on the counter. 'I saw you sitting in your car. And you came in a few minutes after I did.'

'What are you saying?' Glenys's voice rose.

'Just thinking out loud,' said Pippa. 'And yes, if the person who shoved a nail into my tyre wore gloves — which no-one would remark on in February — then fingerprints wouldn't prove anything.' She paused. 'But I can't remember if you came in with gloves on, or not.'

'Jill!' called Glenys. 'If you're not busy…'

'So yes, that's inconclusive.' Pippa scratched her bandaged wrist, carefully. 'But if someone had a chat with Siobhan, and found out she'd run into an acquaintance the day before SingFest, and had a cup of tea with her, before a bad case of upset tummy… And this person had also visited Claire on the day she died, and ensured that Claire was upstairs, while she was left alone with Claire's handbag . . . and Claire's GTN spray . . . which was found to be empty —'

'You're twisting things.' Glenys's hands gripped the counter as if she would break a piece off. 'You're trying to make a crime where no crime exists, like the newspaper said.' She dashed a hand across her eyes. 'Why would I do those things? What would my motive be?'

'Here's one for me,' said Pippa. 'If you did the other two things, then having learnt from the paper what a snooper I am, you'd want me out of the way. You could have killed me — but even if you didn't, then scaring me away from the choir, or putting me out of action for a while, would do.'

'And Siobhan?' Glenys asked, her eyebrows raised.

'Siobhan's quite a character. Easily led, quick to anger and cause trouble. She led the rebel altos on the night when they sabotaged the rehearsal and made Jen so angry — and Claire so upset. But of course you wouldn't want that to happen when the choir had a chance of winning at SingFest UK. So a little something in her tea a day or so beforehand made sense.'

'What about Claire?' Glenys said, through clenched teeth. 'Why would I kill my friend?'

'That was what made this case so difficult,' said Pippa. 'Why would anyone kill Claire? Everyone liked her. She was a mother, a volunteer, a choir member. Not the sort of person who gets killed. But she also wasn't the sort of person to let her angina spray run out.

I thought it might be Pete at first. It's the first place to look, isn't it, the husband or wife. Claire wouldn't give him a divorce, so in that respect a murder made sense. But then it didn't. He was clearly comfortable with the situation, since he could play the field knowing he'd never have to commit. There was no passion there.

That was my task — to find the passion. I found it in two places.

Jen loved Claire. She knew that Claire would never

leave her husband, and would probably never give her the sort of relationship she craved. But she treasured the relationship that they did have.

And then there was you. A devoted friend to Claire for years. Working here together, joining the choir, popping round for chats... You were her closest friend. Perhaps, one day, you hoped for more if you just kept being there.'

Pippa reached into her bag and took out the journal. 'You knew a lot about Claire, but you didn't know that she kept a diary...' Glenys's face drained of colour, and her hands dropped from the counter. 'I only have her last entries, but it's enough.' She replaced the book in her bag.

'When Jen took over the choir, everything changed. Claire was starstruck, and the feeling was mutual. I doubt she told you, but you would have seen it. Of course you would. You tried a few things. First you attempted to convince Claire to leave the choir because of the new music, but there was no way she would do that. Then came the mysterious missing money in this shop. I don't know what you said to Claire to make her feel that leaving was a good idea, but leave she did. That would stop Jen popping into the shop at lunchtimes and after school. You wouldn't have to busy yourself rearranging the displays while you tortured yourself listening to them, watching them...

But you knew from choir, and from the way Claire talked about Jen, that it wasn't over. And you wanted it to finish. You couldn't bear any more.

You'd been cultivating Siobhan and her friends for a while. Dropping hints about Jen, suggesting she played favourites, criticising the music, getting them on side. But something happened to send you over the edge. On the day Claire died, she made a confession to you. Her diary doesn't say exactly what, but from the context . . . I think her relationship with Jen had moved to a deeper level.' Pippa looked steadily at Glenys. 'When she told you, you snapped. You emptied her spray while she was in the bath, and spent the rest of the day getting the altos nicely worked up. They were ready to cause mischief. Jen was angry, Claire was upset. You probably worked on Claire all the way home, so that she was stressed, upset, anxious — in a fine state to have an attack. Pete was away, as usual. He wouldn't be there to phone an ambulance. Claire wouldn't want to wake the children. She reached for her spray — and there was nothing. The shock of that probably killed her.'

Tears ran down Glenys's face, and she made no attempt to stop them. Her shoulders shook a little, but she was calm.

'Do you deny it?' asked Pippa.

Slowly, Glenys shook her head. 'No,' she whispered.

The back door of the shop opened and PC Horsley walked in. He took Glenys gently by the arm. 'There's a car waiting at the side,' he said quietly. 'I'll say the formal bit in the back room.'

Glenys made no resistance as the policeman led her to the door. Jill met them there, her eyes downcast. She closed the door behind them, and the faint deep sound of PC Horsley speaking came through in snatches. No-one spoke until the back door clicked shut, followed a couple of minutes later by a powerful engine stirring to life. No siren, and there would be no blue lights either. A quiet ending.

Jill sighed. 'I would never have believed it.' She surveyed the shop; the racks of clothes, the stacked jigsaws, the plastic toys. 'I won't look at this place in the same way again.'

'If it makes you feel better, I'm not sure she meant to kill her.' Pippa took off the sling and unwound the bandage from her arm, then rubbed it before unclipping her neck collar. 'She might only have meant to frighten her away from the choir. But if she did, it went badly wrong.'

'Didn't it just.' Jill eyed the collar speculatively.

'That reminds me.' Pippa pushed the plastic bag towards her. 'I won't be needing these.'

Jill examined the blouses. 'They are rather horrible,' she admitted.

'They are,' Sheila agreed. 'I can't believe they're on display.'

'Well, if you can do better —' Jill pointed at the *Volunteer* flyers in the rack.

'I tell you what I do need.' Pippa turned to Sheila. 'A strong cup of tea.'

Sheila looked at her watch. 'Haven't you forgotten something?'

Pippa clapped a hand to her mouth. '*Freddie!*' She bundled Sheila out of the shop. 'Much Gadding preschool, and step on it!'

CHAPTER 25

Jen's baton swept to a halt, and Sweet Harmony went with it, ending on a crisp, harmonious high.

A moment of silence, and then applause, whoops, and cheers. Pippa thought she heard Lila's voice. The breath shuddered out of her, and her eyes felt wet when she blinked.

Jen's baton came down slowly, and she smiled at the choir. She looked as if she was about to cry, too. *Well done*, she mouthed, turning to bow to the audience.

Pippa shaded her eyes and peered out. There they were, on the right hand side. Lila, Simon, and Sheila. Simon waved and gave her a thumbs-up. Sheila was pointing at her, speaking to the woman in the next seat. Lila stood up and whistled.

Pippa waved back just before the curtain fell. Siobhan nudged her and they trooped off stage. The next group were waiting to go on, a rainbow of teenage girls in silk shirts.

'Before you go and find your families, gather round,' called Jen.

With some muttering and shuffling, the choir obliged.

Jen tucked her baton into her jacket pocket. 'I want to say thank you. It's been — an odd time. I said things I didn't mean. A lot of us did.' Pippa could feel Siobhan fidgeting beside her. 'Hopefully we're through the worst. I certainly hope so.' She looked at her feet for a moment. 'Whatever happens today, whether we reach the final or not — and let's face it, it's probably not — we did it together. You sang the best you've ever sung. That makes me very proud.' She sniffed, and rubbed her eyes. 'Go and enjoy the rest of it.'

The choir dispersed, chatting. Edie and Daphne stood with Jen, consoling her.

Jen had approached Pippa at the meeting after Glenys's arrest. 'I heard,' she said, simply. 'I'm sorry for the things I said. I thought you were a ghoul, or an ambulance chaser.'

'It's OK,' Pippa muttered.

'It was Glenys who sent me the article,' Jen continued. 'I don't think I can ever forgive her. I doubt she cares about that.' She exhaled, sharply. 'I wonder if —'

'What?'

'I wonder if I was next,' she said abruptly. 'I wouldn't be surprised.'

'I suspected you might be,' said Pippa. 'That's why I moved so quickly. I figured you were probably safe until after SingFest, because she wanted to win, but once that was over…'

'Thank you.' Jen looked bashful. 'It's quite a weird feeling, talking to someone who probably saved your life.'

Pippa's cheeks were heating up. 'S'all right,' she muttered.

'What happened to — was it Sheila?' Jen said, suddenly. 'Didn't she enjoy the choir?'

'I think it was a bit — modern,' Pippa said carefully. Sheila had said much more than that, once the shock of it had worn off, but, well — Jen didn't need to know Sheila's opinion of chart music. Or hippie music. Or miserable medieval composers.

'But you like it, don't you?' Doubt crossed Jen's face. 'I mean, you didn't just keep coming because of —'

'No!' said Pippa. 'I mean, I like some songs more than others, but —'

'Fair enough,' grinned Jen. 'I didn't mean to put you on the spot.' She stuck out a hand. 'Friends?'

'Friends.'

Daphne was hugging Jen now, while Edie contributed a brisk shoulder-rub. *Perhaps I should go to Jen too...* But that would probably bring it all back. And there was somewhere else she needed to be.

Pippa followed the others to the side door, where an usher stood guard. Applause rang out, and he opened it, waving them through. Pippa tried to judge if the noise was more or less enthusiastic than theirs, but she couldn't tell. She climbed the steps of the hall, searching the rows. Suddenly she caught sight of a mop of frizzy blonde hair. Sitting in an aisle seat, in the second row, was Janey Dixon.

'Hello,' said Pippa, sticking out a hand.

Janey Dixon frowned up at her. 'I don't think I —'

'Oh, you do.' Pippa smiled sweetly. 'My name's Pippa Parker. You've written about me. Twice.'

Janey Dixon had the grace to look embarrassed as she shook Pippa's hand with her own bony one. 'Nothing I write is ever meant personally, you know —'

'Actually, I wanted to say thank you.'

Janey Dixon's eyebrows vanished beneath her frizz of hair. 'You wanted to — thank me?'

'Yes.' Pippa recovered her hand. 'You see, if you hadn't written that stupid gossipy article, from which anyone could work out who I was, then Claire Staunton's sister wouldn't have known to give me the vital clue that led to the murderer's arrest.'

Janey Dixon swallowed.

'There is also the point,' said Pippa, her voice rising slightly, 'that the murderer wouldn't have been alerted to my activities, and wouldn't have tried to kill me, too. But hey, swings and roundabouts. I'm sure you'll be more careful in future.' She unleashed one final and she hoped dazzling smile, and strode off to find her family.

'Woo! Here she is!' Lila patted the seat next to her. 'It was great!' She lowered her voice. 'How long does this go on for?'

'Well done, dear.' Sheila leaned across Simon, clapping. 'It actually sounded almost all right.'

'I'll take that as a compliment. Have you got a programme?'

Simon passed his along. 'It was... You were great.'

Pippa examined him. 'Do you really mean that, or are you using your corporate encouragement skills?'

He grinned. 'Not my thing, but great. Will that do?'

'That will do. Ssh, the next lot are coming on.' She ran her finger down the programme. *Oh God.*

'And nowwwwwww...' intoned the MC, 'From the depths of Gadcestershire, iiiiiiiiit's Short Back And Sides!'

'Are they the lot with the motorbike?' whispered Lila.

'That's right,' Pippa whispered back. And the curtain

rose.

Lila snorted. 'They must have crashed the bike. Do they only have one set of clothes?'

'Shut up, Lila,' Pippa hissed. Lila subsided, and gazed obediently at the stage, and Pippa followed suit.

Where was Jeff? She scanned the heads above the leather jackets. *Oh no.* She hadn't scared him off, had she?

Lila nudged her. 'Where's their conductor?' she whispered.

'I don't know,' said Pippa, miserably.

'Maybe he was riding the bike,' Lila sniggered.

A pitch pipe, offstage. As one, the choir began to click their fingers, and the tenors got into gear. 'Hang on, I know this,' muttered Lila. 'It's "Uptown Girl", isn't it?'

'Yes,' whispered Pippa, her heart in her mouth.

A flash of white from the wings, and out came Jeff, fingers snapping, two more T-shirted men following. They strutted to the front of the stage and launched into the melody. Pippa stole a glance at Lila, and held her breath. Lila's eyes were fixed on centre stage.

'They're very good, aren't they,' Sheila said, leaning over again.

'Yes,' said Pippa. 'They are.' She was torn between watching the performance and watching Lila.

'You knew, didn't you?' Lila said, out of the side of her mouth.

Pippa swallowed. 'I saw him at the heats, yes.'

'Explains a few things,' she said. 'I wondered why he hadn't had his hair cut. I told him his fringe was getting ridiculous.'

Pippa eyed Jeff's quiff, which was, admittedly, the highest there. 'Don't be too hard on —'

'Ssshhh.' Lila leaned forward. 'What are they doing?' She was on the edge of her seat, her head bobbing as she tried to get a better view.

'They're moving into the next song.'

'I can't believe you didn't tell me.' Lila shot Pippa an accusing look, but it had a surprising softness at its edges.

'Jeff was worried you wouldn't like it.'

'*Like it?*' Lila turned to the stage, her mouth open. She said nothing for the next two minutes, while the choir poured themselves into 'Never Weather-Beaten Sail'. Pippa thought privately that that must be some sort of record.

The choir held a long, beautiful chord, as they formed into a different shape, a sort of V with Jeff at the centre. 'Woah,' murmured Lila. '*Woah.*'

'Ooh, now this is good.' Sheila settled in her seat. 'Unchained whatsits. Is it the Thankful Brothers?'

'Righteous Brothers, Mum,' Simon said, wearily.

The simple arpeggios rang out, the choir as piano. Jeff looked slightly nervous. *At least he doesn't know Lila's here.* He breathed deeply, stepped forward, and sang.

'Oh my God.' Lila was craning to see. 'I can't — I can't —' She stood up. Pippa tugged on her top to make her sit, but she wouldn't budge.

Jeff was facing the crowd, singing his heart out.

'Sit down!' hissed someone in the row behind.

Jeff's eyes shifted towards them, and widened. His voice wobbled a fraction. A tiny fraction.

Lila scrambled past Pippa to the aisle.

Jeff kept singing, the notes pouring out, his eyes fixed on Lila.

'Does she need the toilet?' Sheila whispered.

'Sshh,' Pippa murmured. 'I think it's going to be all right.'

'That's a relief,' said Sheila. 'It's terrible when you have to hold it in, isn't it?'

The song was drawing to a close. Jeff, still singing, beckoned with a finger.

Lila walked down the stairs as if she was in a trance. Jeff hit the final high note square on. Pippa breathed. *Don't wreck it, Jeff. A few more notes, and you're there.*

Lila reached the foot of the stage as Jeff began the last line, and headed for the steps at the side. Jeff walked to meet her. As he ended his last note, Lila ran up the steps and threw herself into his arms.

The choir were singing the last few notes, but no-one cared. The audience was on its feet.

'Does Lila know that young man?' Sheila asked.

'You could say that,' said Pippa, applauding.

'We have a pitch invasionnn!' the MC declared. Jeff and Lila stood for a moment, looking into each other's eyes.

And then he kissed her.

'I can't believe you set that up, Pippa,' Simon grinned.

'I didn't!'

'Yeah, right.' But he was beaming. 'He's quite the showman, isn't he?'

'Only on stage,' said Pippa, as the curtain fell.

'Do you think Lila's coming back?' Sheila asked.

'I doubt it,' said Pippa. 'They've probably gone to find a potter's wheel.'

'I beg your pardon?'

'I'll explain later. We should probably go, anyway.'

'What, and not find out who won?' Sheila said

indignantly.

'I think we know who's won,' Pippa grinned. 'We ought to head home. It was sweet of Marge to mind the kids, but both at the same time…' She sighed. 'I guess it's back to normal now.'

'Normal,' snorted Sheila. 'I'll believe it when I see it.' And she gave Pippa a wide, conspiratorial smile.

ACKNOWLEDGEMENTS

My first thanks and several gold stars go to my beta readers — Ruth Cunliffe, Paula Harmon, and Stephen Lenhardt — and to my proofreader, medical advisor, and musical expert, John Croall. They have all done a wonderful job in super-quick time — guess who wanted to get one more book done before the end of the year! Any errors which remain are, of course, down to me.

More thanks to the Bold Street Writers, who have again had to put up with getting selected chunks of the story at our weekly write-ins, and also, occasionally, becoming part of the story (hello Eileen!). Let's do it all again next year.

Another thank you goes to members of the Facebook Cozy and Traditional Mystery Writers group for their helpful cover critique, and especially Pam Martin for her singing snowmen suggestion! You can find out more about Pam at http://sassyscribblerpjm.wixsite.com/sassyscribbler.

Big big thanks to (here he is again) my husband Stephen, who is not only very supportive of my writing, but also a much better cook than either Simon or Pippa.

My final thanks go to you, the reader. I hope you've enjoyed the latest instalment of Pippa's adventures. If you have, please consider leaving a short review of *Murder in the Choir* on Amazon or Goodreads. As I now have four — four! — book series on the go, I'm trying to prioritise which series I publish in next by their review rating. So if you want the next Pippa book soon, review this one!

FONT AND IMAGE CREDITS

Fonts:

MURDER font: Edo Regular by Vic Fieger (freeware): www.fontsquirrel.com/fonts/Edo

Classic font: Nimbus Roman No9 L by URW++: www.fontsquirrel.com/fonts/nimbus-roman-no9-l.
License — GNU General Public License v2.00: https://www.fontsquirrel.com/license/nimbus-roman-no9-l

Script font: Dancing Script OT by Impallari Type: www.fontsquirrel.com/fonts/dancing-script-ot. License — SIL Open Font License v.1.10: http://scripts.sil.org/OFL

Vector graphics:

Apart from the footsteps (by Angela Su at clker.com), all vectors used are from www.vecteezy.com

Cover created using GIMP image editor: www.gimp.org.

ABOUT THE AUTHOR

Liz Hedgecock grew up in London, England, did an English degree, and then took forever to start writing. After several years working in the National Health Service, a corporate writing course rekindled the flame, and various short stories followed. Some even won prizes. The stories started to grow longer — and then the murders began . . .

Liz's reimaginings of Sherlock Holmes, *Murder at the Playgroup* (first in the Pippa Parker series), and *Bitesize*, a flash fiction collection, are available in ebook and paperback.

Liz now lives in Cheshire with her husband and two sons, and when she's not writing or child-wrangling you can usually find her reading, messing about on Twitter, or cooing over stuff in museums and art galleries.

Website/blog: http://lizhedgecock.wordpress.com
Facebook: http://www.facebook.com/lizhedgecockwrites
Twitter: http://twitter.com/lizhedgecock
Goodreads: https://www.goodreads.com/lizhedgecock

OTHER BOOKS BY LIZ HEDGECOCK

Short stories

The Secret Notebook of Sherlock Holmes
Bitesize

Halloween Sherlock series (novelettes)

The Case of the Snow-White Lady
Sherlock Holmes and the Deathly Fog

Sherlock & Jack series (novellas)

A Jar Of Thursday
Something Blue

Mrs Hudson & Sherlock Holmes series (novels)

A House Of Mirrors
In Sherlock's Shadow (2018)

Pippa Parker Mysteries (novels)

Murder At The Playgroup
Murder In The Choir

Pippa Parker will return in
A Fete Worse Than **DEATH**

Pippa Parker Mysteries: 3

WHITE RHINO BOOKS

Printed in Great Britain
by Amazon